Tales from Grace Chapel Inn

Spring *Is* in the *Air*

JANE ORCUTT

D0088447

Guideposts
New York, New York

Spring Is in the Air

ISBN-13: 978-0-8249-4759-0

Published by Guideposts
16 East 34th Street
New York, New York 10016
www.guideposts.com

Distributed by Ideals Publications
2636 Elm Hill Pike, Suite 120
Nashville, TN 37214

Guideposts, Ideals and *Tales from Grace Chapel Inn* are registered trademarks of Guideposts.

The characters and events in this book are fictional, and any resemblance to actual persons or events is coincidental.

All Scripture quotations are taken from *The Holy Bible, New International Version.* Copyright © 1973, 1978, 1984 International Bible Society. Used by permission of Zondervan Bible Publishers.

Library of Congress Cataloging-in-Publication Data

Orcutt, Jane.
  Spring is in the air / Jane Orcutt.
    p. cm.—(Tales from Grace Chapel Inn)
  ISBN 978-0-8249-4759-0
  1. Sisters—Fiction. 2. Bed and breakfast accommodations—Fiction.
3. Community life—Pennsylvania—Fiction. 4. Pennsylvania—Social life
and customs—Fiction. 5. Domestic fiction. I. Title.
  PS3565.R37S67 2009
  813'.54—dc22

                                         2008024139

Cover by Deborah Chabrian
Design by Marisa Jackson
Typeset by Nancy Tardi

Printed and bound in the United States of America

10 9 8 7 6 5 4 3 2 1

Spring Is in the Air

To Colin and Sam, first-class cardboard-boat builders and sailors.

GRACE CHAPEL INN

A place where one can be
refreshed and encouraged,
a place of hope and healing,
a place where God is at home.

Chapter One

*W*hat dost thee think of this?"

Ethel Buckley stood in the kitchen of Grace Chapel Inn, a flat straw hat perched on her head. Even though she was in her seventies, she was still vain enough to dye her hair, and a bit of bottled red peeked out beneath the straw brim. More than one of her three Howard nieces, seated at the table, had to smother a smile. They were accustomed to their elderly aunt popping in through the back door to their cozy bed-and-breakfast, and they were also accustomed to her spirited antics. But none of them was prepared for the sight of their aunt impersonating an Amish woman.

"I believe that hats are worn by men," Louise Howard Smith said tactfully. The oldest of the three sisters, she was as practical in her speech as she was in demeanor. "Women wear white caps."

Ethel removed the hat, a look of disappointment crossing her face.

"Not that yours doesn't look wonderful," Alice Howard added. "But I do believe Louise is right." The middle sister,

Alice avoided confrontation as much as possible and sought to encourage others when she could.

Jane Howard, the youngest and most outspoken of the three, didn't mince words. "I think you're talking more like a Quaker anyway. I don't think the Amish use words like *thee* and *thou*. Where in the world did you get that hat, Auntie? And why are you wearing it today?"

"I bought two. I thought it would be fun for you and Sylvia Songer to wear them for your trip to Pennsylvania Dutch country," Ethel said. "To help you both get in the spirit."

"Oh, Auntie, you are so sweet, but I don't think we need any help in looking forward to the trip," Jane said. She set a plate of Reuben sandwiches on the table along with a bowl of homemade potato salad. The cook of the family, as well as of the inn, she prided herself on making everything as natural and as fresh as possible. No store-bought sandwiches or side dishes in *her* kitchen.

"Sit down and join us for lunch, Aunt Ethel," Alice said, rising to get another plate from the cabinet. "Would you like milk, lemonade—"

"Lemonade would be lovely." Ethel took a seat at the table. "I'm sorry you don't care for my hat idea."

Jane shot Alice and Louise a look while she set a glass pitcher of lemonade on the table. The sisters were as different in appearance as they were in nature. Alice had bobbed reddish-brown hair and brown eyes, while Jane had long, dark hair, fair skin and blue eyes. She and Louise had inherited their father's height. Louise had short silver hair, blue eyes and pale skin. Louise was a widow; Jane a divorcée, and Alice had chosen the single life. Together they had renovated and opened their family home in Acorn Hill, Pennsylvania, as Grace Chapel Inn.

"Even if it's only a hat, I don't think Sylvia and I are the dressing-alike types," Jane said.

"I don't believe Mother ever dressed Louise and me alike when we were children," Alice said. Both in their sixties, she and her older sister were only three years apart. Jane was the baby of the family, twelve years younger than Alice. She never knew their mother, Madeleine Howard, who had died during Jane's birth.

"Thank you, dear," Ethel said, accepting a glass of lemonade from Louise. "No, I don't believe she did. Madeleine loved to dress you girls up, but she believed that children should have their own identities. She believed in individuality —something that Jane seems to have in abundance." She smiled at her youngest niece over the rim of the glass.

"Hats or no hats, I am delighted, Jane, that you and Sylvia are taking this trip," Louise said.

"Me too," Jane said. "I haven't been to Lancaster in a long time. It might as well be three states over instead of nearby. Sylvia was nice to invite me along for her quilt-buying expedition. I'm not as knowledgeable about quilts as she is, but I like looking at any handmade items." Jane took her normal seat at the table and put half a sandwich onto her plate. "And eating good home cooking, for which the Amish country is famous."

"I think that it'll be fun, too, to be a guest in someone else's home," Alice said, her eyes twinkling. "It's nice to *be* a guest sometimes, to remind yourself of what guests experience."

Jane looked thoughtful. "It will be interesting to stay with Sylvia's friends, but I'll miss you all. I wish you were going with us."

"Someone has to keep the home fires burning," Alice said.

"And take care of Wendell," Louise said, referring to the gray tabby cat who had been a favorite of their late father.

"It's been a long time since I visited Lancaster too," Alice said. "I suppose the women still sell their homemade delicacies and handiwork in the stores."

"I doubt that much has changed. Life does not alter much for the Amish," Louise said, eyes twinkling. "They are not much for innovation."

"Or modern conveniences," Jane agreed.

Alice smiled. "I've always found the Amish way of life attractive. The families seem to remain close to each other—emotionally and physically. And there's none of the hurry-up mentality that's so prevalent in our world."

"Life is definitely slower there," Louise said. "But I don't think I could manage without electricity or automobiles for very long. I'm afraid that I'm quite spoiled."

"Oh, I could do it," Jane said. "It'd be a snap. Think of the gardening. Think of the fresh food."

"Think of the long skirts," Alice said, chuckling. "That's what always stops me from daydreaming too long."

Ethel, who had been eating her sandwich with gusto, swallowed and dabbed her mouth with her napkin. "I agree with Alice. It sounds like a fun way to live, until you actually have to do it. I remember what it was like not to have a car."

"Aunt Ethel, you can't possibly be old enough to remember horse-and-buggy days," Jane said.

"*Tsk*, of course not. When I was very young, though, not everyone owned an automobile. You either hitched a ride with someone who did, or you walked everywhere."

"See?" Jane said. "I could do that. After all, I like to jog." She propped her chin in her hand. "I wonder if the Amish allow running shoes."

"If you don't collect Sylvia and get on the road, you'll never find out," Alice said, then she volunteered to clean up the dishes while Jane went upstairs to gather her things. Louise went to help Jane, leaving Alice and Ethel alone in the kitchen.

Ethel started gathering the dishes, sighing heavily as she carried them to the sink.

"Is there anything wrong, Aunt Ethel?" Alice asked.

Ethel started running water to rinse the plates before putting them in the dishwasher. "I envy Jane and Sylvia, I guess."

"I'm sure Lloyd would take you to the Amish country if you wanted," Alice said. Lloyd Tynan was Acorn Hill's elderly mayor. He and Ethel had been sweet on each other for a long time, and he was a good friend to the sisters as well. He and Ethel occasionally took day trips together to sightsee.

"I know that Lloyd would take me," Ethel said. "I think I'm just feeling a little bored lately, a little bit in a rut, I guess." She scrubbed a dish thoughtfully.

Alice put an arm around her aunt. "Maybe you need a new hobby. Something to give you a change of pace."

"Perhaps." Ethel brightened. "Don't trouble yourself about it, Alice. I'm sure I'll be fine. Maybe you're right. I just need something new to do."

Jane pulled up at Sylvia's small dressmaker's shop, Sylvia's Buttons, on Acorn Avenue. Sylvia was already outside the building, her small leather suitcase beside her on the sidewalk.

Jane got out of Louise's old but well-maintained Cadillac and opened the trunk for Sylvia's suitcase. "I'm so excited,"

Sylvia said, her dark eyes shining. "I've been so eager for this trip that I could hardly sleep last night."

"I've been looking forward to it too," Jane said, giving her friend a hug. "Thanks for inviting me to go with you."

"Well thank you, Jane, for driving," Sylvia said. "I don't mind going by myself, but it's much more fun to have a friend along. Particularly when she volunteers the use of her sister's car."

"Don't thank me, thank Louise. She was kind enough to lend me her Caddy. It has much better trunk space than either of our cars. You might need the room if you find lots to buy."

They got into the car. Before Jane started the ignition, she looked at Sylvia and smiled. "What are you thinking?" she asked.

"Probably the same thing you are," Sylvia said.

"Road trip!" they said at the same time.

Jane turned the key and revved the engine. She and Sylvia then headed down the road laughing.

Winter had given way to spring. Though it was mid-May, the temperature was almost summerlike. Buttercups and orange daylilies bloomed alongside the road, highlighting the way.

Jane sighed.

"What is it?" Sylvia asked.

"It's nice to get away for a night," Jane said. "I love Grace Chapel Inn and Acorn Hill. And I *certainly* love Louise and Alice. But it's nice to go somewhere else occasionally."

"All the way into the big county of Lancaster," Sylvia teased.

"Hey, it's an adventure. And you know I'm *always* up for that."

Leaving the highway, Jane took a more rural route to their destination. They passed small towns and Amish farms. Lines of wash were hanging near the farm houses. Dresses of various shades of blue or purple fluttered on one line, while another held rows of men's and boys' solid-color shirts and overalls. Red barns dotted the green fields. The farmhouses themselves seemed exceptionally neat and trim. White was the paint color of choice, but some houses were a hodge-podge of white and red paints, and even aged wood, like a crazy quilt.

"Why do some of the houses look like that?" Jane asked.

"Because the original house is frequently added on to," Sylvia said. "Families grow and need more space. Children marry and need extra room. People age and so rooms are built for them."

"Very practical," Jane said, "and loving."

Though they had yet to come up behind a horse-drawn buggy that the Amish were famous for driving, several passed on the other side of the wide-shouldered road. Some buggies were driven by children, others by women, and a few were driven by clean-shaven young men. Jane knew that they were unmarried men, for only Amish husbands grew beards.

"If you get behind a buggy, be careful," Sylvia said. "It takes a lot of patience to drive a car in these parts. Sometimes you have to wait a long time to pass the buggies. I've seen traffic at a standstill just waiting for the lead car to pass on these country roads."

"I'll be careful," Jane promised. She pointed out that the fields looked ready for plowing. "What do they plant around here mostly? Sweet corn?"

Sylvia nodded. "Some tobacco too."

They had agreed to head to the home of Sylvia's friend first. They would be spending the night there. With Sylvia giving directions, Jane headed down one side road after another until they saw a sign that said Maple Grove Hall.

"Turn here," Sylvia said.

"They named their home?"

Sylvia smiled. "Their home isn't a bed-and-breakfast or anything, but it seemed appropriate. Look around you."

The road leading to the house was lined on both sides with stately maples.

"Wow!" Jane said. "I'm impressed."

"The house is surrounded by Amish farms. It's nice to wake up to the sound of horses clip-clopping along with their buggies."

"Your friends aren't Amish, are they?" Jane asked.

Sylvia shook her head. "Their parents were Mennonites, but they don't consider themselves such. They do practice a plain life, though." She smiled. "But don't worry, they have electricity and all the modern conveniences."

"I could live an Amish lifestyle," Jane said.

"Sure you could," Sylvia said amiably. "One day with plain cookware and you'd be howling for your food processor and fancy oven."

Jane laughed. "You're probably right."

At Sylvia's direction, Jane pulled alongside the house, a two-story gray limestone.

"There's Fenella!" Sylvia hopped out of the car and headed for the porch. A fiftyish, plump woman with a ruddy complexion and thick gray hair waited at the top of the porch stairs, wiping her flour-dusted hands on a starched white apron. She pulled Sylvia into a hug.

"Fenella!" Sylvia said, smiling. "It's been far too long."

"It has indeed," Fenella said, then pulled back to wag her finger. "I know you come to this area primarily to shop for quilts and quilting materials, but I like to think you stop in here occasionally just to see me."

"You know I do," Sylvia said, feigning shock. She drew Jane toward Fenella. "As promised, I brought a friend with me this time. Fenella Hoppenstedt, meet Jane Howard."

"It's good to meet you," Jane said, holding out her hand. To her surprise, Fenella pulled her into a warm hug.

"Any friend of Sylvia's is a friend of mine," Fenella said. "I'm so glad you could both come. Would you like to get settled before you head out for the day?"

"That's a good idea," Sylvia said.

She and Jane got their bags from the car and followed Fenella inside. "Sylvia tells me you run a bed-and-breakfast," Fenella said. "I'm sure your home is bigger, but we think our place is snug enough."

"It's beautiful," Jane said, passing through the entryway. Simple rugs adorned the hardwood floors in the living area, which had a worn but comfortable-looking love seat and sofa, and handcrafted tables and bookcases.

"This home was built in the late 1700s by Elijah's ancestors," Fenella said proudly, glancing around the room. "It was made to last, that's for certain. If you'll follow me, we'll go upstairs."

When they reached the landing, she explained, "We have only one guest room, which you two will be sharing. Again, it's not big, but it's homey."

She opened the door to a small room. A four-poster bed covered with a chenille spread dominated the space. A four-drawer dresser, a simple floor lamp, and small nightstands on either side of the bed completed the furnishings.

"The bathroom's across the hall," Fenella said. "I hope you don't have any trouble getting in and out of the tub. It's a claw foot, and you have to be careful since it's so high off the ground. As for amenities like TVs, VCRs or even clock radios, I'm afraid we don't have them. I'm sure you're accustomed to fancy things, Jane, since you run an inn of your own."

Sylvia laughed. "They don't have most of those things at their place either. The Howard sisters practice their own form of simple living, and that's one of the reasons that Grace Chapel Inn is so popular. People go there to unwind and get away from the hustle and bustle."

"Then you'll feel at home here," Fenella said. "I'll let you unpack. Just let me know if you need anything. After you get settled, come downstairs and I'll make some tea."

Jane glanced around the spartan room. Windows on two walls provided views of a young crop field on one side and a road on the other. Beyond the road, she could see what must be an Amish house, with four rows of dark pants hanging on the line outside. A tidy garden nestled near the plain white house, and Jane could see a woman with a white cap working the soil, getting ready for planting.

Jane enjoyed the view. Gardening transcended all cultures.

Sylvia stood beside her, watching over her shoulder. "That's Rachel King."

"I wonder what she plants," Jane said, mostly to herself.

"Lots of vegetables, I'm certain," Sylvia said. "She and Fenella are the best of friends. They discuss gardening a lot."

Jane turned away from the window. "Do you suppose she considers gardening a chore?"

"I've talked to Mrs. King several times, and she and Fenella are good friends for a good reason. They both adhere to Colossians 3:23, which says 'Whatever you do, work at it with all your heart, as working for the Lord, not for men.' I'm sure she considers it a joy."

Jane smiled. "Sounds like my kind of woman."

Chapter Two

After Jane and Sylvia unpacked, they headed downstairs. Fenella put on the teakettle to boil, and the three settled on the sofa and love seat in the living room.

"Is Elijah in town?" Sylvia asked.

Fenella nodded. "He's still at the store." She turned to Jane. "We own and operate a pretzel-making store. They're very popular with the tourists." She winked. "Even some of the locals have been known to eat them from time to time."

The kettle whistled. Fenella excused herself and ducked into the kitchen. When she returned, she had a tray laden with a teapot, cups, saucers and an assortment of cookies.

Jane selected one and bit into it. "*Mmm.* Oatmeal raisin. And still warm too. This is wonderful."

"Thank you," Fenella said. "I try to bake a fresh batch of cookies every day. Elijah and I like a cookie now and then, but I bake them more for anyone who might drop by or to give to Rachel King and her family next door."

"We saw her working in her garden," Sylvia said. "Are the Kings doing well?"

Fenella nodded. "All seventeen of them."

Jane looked surprised. "I've heard the Amish have large families, but fifteen kids?"

Fenella chuckled. "Only thirteen. Rachel's parents live with them as well. So, speaking of the Amish, what plans do you two have while you're in Lancaster County? Sightseeing?"

"A little," Sylvia told her. "But mostly we came to see my friend Roma. She has some new quilts to show me. One of the local women brings them in for her to sell in her antiques shop. She gives some to me on consignment so that I can sell them in my shop back in Acorn Hill."

"I love Roma's shop," Fenella said. "Who quilts for her?"

"Hannah Stoltzfus."

Fenella shook her head in wonder. "I don't know how she manages, being a widow with all those children. I figured she would remarry by now. Well, it's a blessing that she can make some money at Roma's. The Amish don't need much, but a body has to have some income."

"I understand the Amish take good care of each other," Jane said.

"Indeed they do. We outsiders would do well to learn from them."

"I think we do pretty well in Acorn Hill," Sylvia said, "but then again, we live in a small town. I'm sure it's difficult in a larger area. Is Hannah Stoltzfus being looked after?"

Fenella nodded. "She has two grown sons to begin with. So they help out. As do the children still at home, of course. The Amish are very close-knit, not only in their practices, but in their hearts as well. The *Ordnung* is the set of rules that they live by, but legalism isn't the key with them." She smiled. "But here, I didn't mean to lecture. You're not here to gawk at the plain people as so many tourists are."

Sylvia set her empty tea cup in its saucer. "What *would* you like to do today, Jane? I come here so often, I've seen just about everything."

"I'd just love to drive around the area," she said. "Then remember, I promised you a nice dinner out tonight. Something fancy. Fenella, Roma is coming. Will you and your husband join us too?"

"Thank you, dear, but Elijah and I are simple folk who eat simply. I'm afraid any fancy foods would be wasted on us. You go out tonight and enjoy yourselves. I understand there are several very good gourmet restaurants in the area."

Jane nodded. "I've done a little research, and there are some highly recommended ones. I'm sorry you don't want to join us, but I understand." She set her cup and saucer beside Sylvia's on the tray. "The tea and cookies were lovely, Fenella."

Their hostess smiled. "You better run along if you're going to see Roma's *and* some of the area while it's still daylight. I'll see you whenever you come back here. Be sure to stop in the store. Elijah will make sure that you sample a pretzel or two."

Jane patted her stomach and looked at Sylvia. "I can already tell that this area is going to be dangerous to my waistline."

They drove toward Roma's shop. This time Sylvia was at the wheel, because she knew her way around Lancaster so well. Still, they both oohed and ahhed over the sights—Lancaster had everything from quaint stores to gourmet restaurants to parks.

"There's a renaissance fair in the area during the fall," Sylvia said, pointing out sites and describing events like a tour guide. "And also a hot-air-balloon festival."

"That sounds like fun," Jane said.

"In 1777 Lancaster was even the capital of the United States for one day, when the Congress fled the British in Philadelphia," Sylvia continued.

Tucked away from the hustle and bustle of the tourist area was a small gray shop whose sign announced Roma's Antiques. "It's a bit off the beaten path, but her shop is well known and buyers have learned to seek her out," Sylvia said.

"Looks like she sells quite a variety of old things," Jane said as Sylvia parked the car in front. On the front porch was an old bicycle, a child's wagon and an ancient typewriter.

"My father used to type on one of those," Jane said as they passed it on their way into the store.

A short woman with dark hair pulled back in a bun opened her arms when she saw them. "Sylvia Songer! Look at you!"

They embraced. Sylvia introduced Jane, then said, "And this is Roma Tobias."

"I've heard so much about you," Roma said. "I know you're both staying with Fenella. How do you like her home? She's way out there in the country."

"It's wonderful." Jane glanced around the store. "Just like your place. I've never seen such a collection."

Roma laughed. "Would you like to browse while Sylvia and I talk?"

"Actually, I'm eager to see what you have for her," Jane said.

Roma nodded. "Let's have a look at the quilts then."

They followed her past aisles of antique Amish and Shaker furniture, curiously mixed among fifty-year-old metal service-station signs and early-model blenders and hand mixers.

"I need to tidy that spot," she said. "It doesn't look good to have that beautiful furniture flanked with reminders of the items that the Amish themselves never use. Here we are."

She stopped in front of a tall, deep-grained wooden armoire, which she opened to reveal quilts neatly stacked on three shelves. "The latest ones I've received are on this shelf," she said, taking a few off the top. She took them over to a low table and spread them out.

Jane marveled at the intricate handwork. One had a blue-and-white diamond pattern, with each white diamond containing four different-colored hearts. Another had green and white squares, each white square holding a multicolored flower. Still another had what Roma said was a lone-star pattern, with shades of green, burgundy and floral accents against an ivory background.

"If you look closely, you can see the faint pencil lines where the intricate pattern was marked and hand stitched," Roma said.

Jane studied the quilt, admiring the small, precise stitches.

The front door opened, and a young Amish woman entered. She wore a dark dress and a starched white cap over her hair, which was pulled back in a bun. "Hello, Miss Tobias, I—" She stopped short when she saw Jane and Sylvia.

"Annie," Roma said, all smiles as she moved toward her visitor, "these are friends of mine visiting from Acorn Hill. You already know Miss Songer."

"Of course. How are you, Miss Songer?" Annie said, smiling at Sylvia.

"It's good to see you again, Annie. It has been a year or two. How old are you now?" Sylvia asked.

"Seventeen."

"That's a great age," Jane said, then introduced herself.

"And this is Annie Stoltzfus," Roma said. "Annie, they are here to look at quilts. I was just showing them some of your mother's."

"Your mother made these?" Jane asked.

"She had some help," Annie said pleasantly. "I even helped a little, though mostly it was the older women who did the work."

"Do you help out with the sewing after school?" Jane asked.

"Oh no, ma'am," Annie said. "We only go through eighth grade. I finished several years ago. Mostly I help my mam around the house. I have five younger brothers and sisters."

"You have older brothers, right?"

"Yes, ma'am. I'm the oldest still at home. I have two older brothers and one sister. They're already married."

Roma patted the quilt draped over her arm. "Annie keeps busy. She also comes to visit me, bringing her mother's quilts for sale. Annie, Miss Songer is hoping to take a few back with her to Acorn Hill to sell there."

"Where is Acorn Hill?" she asked.

"About an hour west of Philadelphia," Sylvia said.

Annie shook her head. "I've always wanted to go to Philadelphia. Especially when we were studying the American Revolution. There must be so much to see in the city."

"Philadelphia, yes. Acorn Hill, no," Jane said. "It's a small town, Annie. Smaller than Lancaster, even."

"Lancaster feels plenty big when it's tourist season. Like now." She clapped her hand over her mouth. "I didn't mean that we don't want you here. I'm always happy to see Miss Songer. And now you, of course, Miss Howard."

"I'm also interested in your mother's quilts," Jane said. "She and her friends do beautiful work. Are all the quilts in your home like this?"

Annie shook her head. "These are just for show. And to sell. Oh, Miss Tobias, I'm so *fergesslich!* I almost forgot to give you the message from Mam. She said to tell you that she would have another quilt for you tomorrow, if you're interested."

"So soon? That's wonderful, Annie. Tell your mother thank you."

Annie bobbed her white-capped head. "It was nice to meet you, Miss Howard, and to see you again, Miss Songer."

"It was nice to meet you too, Annie," Jane said.

"Will we be seeing you at lunch tomorrow?" Sylvia asked the girl.

"Oh yes, I wouldn't miss that," Annie replied shyly. Then she gave the group a little wave and was off.

Jane turned to Roma. "She's lovely. What will her future be like, Roma?"

"She'll marry in a year or two and start having children of her own, no doubt."

"Does she have a choice?"

"She hasn't been baptized yet, but once she is, she must stay with the Amish and obey their teachings. And that is to be separate from the world."

"What if she doesn't obey?"

"If she's baptized, then she'll be shunned. The Amish consider shunning the last form of love they can offer to bring an errant person to correction."

"But what if she's not baptized?" Jane asked.

"Then of course she's free to go her own way in the world. Though with the way they're brought up, surrounded by family and church, it's not a path that many Amish choose. The pull to remain is just too strong. It's the only life they know."

"The Amish lifestyle is difficult for me to understand," Jane admitted.

"It is for a lot of people," Roma said. "The Amish give up things that we take for granted like electricity and cars, but they gain tighter-knit families, a much lower level of crime and, I believe, a deeper sense of walking day to day with God."

"But what about higher education? What about seeing the world beyond their own four corners?" Jane asked. "Are they missing out?"

"That," Roma said, "is a question you would have to ask them."

Roma put the quilts away, including the ones Sylvia selected to take with her back to Acorn Hill. She would pick them up the next day before they returned home.

While Roma took care of some paperwork in the back of the store, Jane and Sylvia browsed the shop. When Roma was finished, she closed the store and they all got into the car with Sylvia behind the wheel and Roma beside her as the navigator. Jane sat in the back seat.

"I know a wonderful place to eat," Roma said. "Jane, Sylvia told me to pick out something gourmet, since that is your interest. I chose Dunstan's, which is owned by an old friend who doubles as the chef. Many people think the Pennsylvania Dutch country is only about down-home country cooking, but we have several four- and five-star restaurants as well. Dunstan's is one of them."

"Sounds wonderful," Jane said, settling back contentedly as Sylvia drove toward the restaurant. Jane was always excited about trying a new gourmet restaurant. As a former chef at a well-known San Francisco restaurant, she had a professional interest in fine food.

Her heart sank when she saw Dunstan's, a nondescript stone-and-brick building with a humble carved wood sign over the front door announcing the restaurant's name.

Sylvia looked in the rearview mirror and caught sight of Jane's expression. "Don't be fooled. The atmosphere inside and the food are wonderful. Roma made a good selection for you."

Once inside, Jane had to agree. A welcoming ambience was created by candlelight and soft classical music. Thick folk-art carpets covered the floor, and paintings by local artists lined the softly lit walls. Creamy damask tablecloths covered each table. As the maître d' led the party to a back room, Jane sighed happily.

Sometimes she missed the restaurant business. She would never leave Grace Chapel Inn or her sisters, of course, but she missed the hustle and bustle that she knew was occurring even now back in the kitchen while the customers chatted quietly over their meals.

Once the menu was in her hand, she studied it, looking for clues to the chef's strengths and weaknesses. The menu seemed to be tailored to an older, middle-class clientele who liked familiarity in their food selections. Nothing wrong with that, particularly in a tourist town like Lancaster.

Sylvia shut her menu. "It's a tough call, but I think I'll go with the salmon Wellington."

"I'm choosing fish too," Roma said. "The trout almandine. Jane?"

"Filet of beef with peppercorns," she said.

When Jane's entrée arrived, she was impressed by its presentation. The perfectly cooked filet, crusted with three kinds of peppercorns, was centered on her plate. Creamy mashed potatoes were piped around it, and these were accented by rosettes of pureed carrots. The other entrées were also artfully served. More important, each woman pronounced her entrée delicious.

Mindful of their waistlines, they decided to share a serving of pear tart. The rich, flaky crust and tender, caramelized fruit was a delightful finale to their meal.

They left the restaurant and dropped Roma at her home, then returned to Fenella's. It was nearly nine o'clock, and though she and Elijah had already retired, Fenella had left the front door unlocked for them.

"They keep daylight hours, much like the Amish," Sylvia explained.

Soon Jane and Sylvia were settled under the covers of the featherbed. "Ohhh, I ate too much," Jane whispered into the darkness. "But every morsel was worth it. Promise you won't let me ever eat again, okay, Sylvia?"

Sylvia laughed softly. "I can't do that. We're having lunch with Hannah and her family tomorrow."

Jane groaned. "I understand the Amish eat hearty."

"They do physical work all day. They have to eat a lot."

"*Hmm.* If I were Amish, I could eat a big meal every day and work it off."

Sylvia's voice sounded drowsy as she replied, "You have a lot in common with them. You'll see when you talk to Hannah tomorrow."

Chapter Three

*T*he next morning, Jane and Sylvia rose early. They took turns in the guest bathroom, dressed and headed downstairs promptly at seven o'clock.

"Good morning." Fenella greeted them with a bright face. "I have breakfast waiting for you in the kitchen."

As they followed Fenella, Sylvia whispered to Jane. "I know you never want to eat again, but you'll need your strength today. We've got a busy schedule."

"Part of which includes lunch," Jane whispered back.

They entered the kitchen, which had cream-colored walls and dark wooden cabinets. Fenella had a light breakfast laid out for them on the round wooden table.

"Just scrambled eggs, grits, fruit and juice this morning," Fenella said. "If I know Hannah Stoltzfus, she'll have a large lunch for you, and I'm sure you don't want to fill up beforehand. How was your dinner last night?"

"We went to Dunstan's," Sylvia said, "and the food was wonderful."

"It was magnificent," Jane agreed, "in both preparation and presentation."

"The presentation won't be fancy at Hannah's, but the preparation will be excellent, I'm sure," Fenella said.

"I'm sure it will," Sylvia said. "Hannah makes the best fried chicken I've ever had," she said, then caught herself when she saw Jane arch her eyebrow. "I mean *some* of the best fried chicken."

After they had eaten and thanked Fenella, they got into the car.

"Let's do some sightseeing and shopping before lunch. Sound good?" Sylvia asked.

"Sounds very good," Jane said. "I'll drive if you tell me where to go."

"Let's take the scenic route so that you can see more of the countryside," Sylvia said.

Once again they saw Amish buggies on the road, and Jane braked carefully before passing them.

"Why are some buggies black and some gray?" Jane asked. "It's not a status symbol, is it?"

"Among the Amish? No. The buggies are different colors only to symbolize what particular group they're with. In other areas of Pennsylvania, the buggies may have white or yellow tops. Here in Lancaster County, the Old Order Amish drive gray buggies, and the Old Order Mennonites drive black."

"And the difference between Amish and Mennonites is . . ."

"They both have the same sixteenth-century roots, and both believe in the same Christian doctrine," Sylvia said. "Basically, the Amish are more strict in their outward separation from the world."

Jane felt as if *she* were in another world. The countryside was quiet, and the roads were narrow. Jane almost wished that she were driving a buggy, so that she could enjoy the scenery at a slower pace.

They passed a multitude of farms, then Sylvia pointed out a white-painted one-room school. All the students in their caps or straw hats gamboled on a green field, apparently at recess.

They crossed several covered bridges, and Sylvia said that many in the county were built in the nineteenth century. She advised Jane to drive slowly when they crossed.

"I've always wondered why some bridges are covered," Jane said.

"My understanding is that it's to protect the trusses from bad weather," Sylvia said. "The bridges are a big attraction for tourists."

"I can see why. There's a certain romantic quality about them."

Jane studied a road sign they passed. "There certainly are a lot of little towns in this county. Ephrata, Lititz, Bird-in-Hand..."

"Yes, there are. We'll try to visit as many in this area as we can before lunch and finish up afterward."

She directed Jane to different towns, where they got out and shopped. Most of them were like Lancaster, obviously catering to tourists. Tourists were easy to recognize for they often stopped to stare at the Amish women and men going about their business. Jane knew that the Amish did not like to be photographed, believing those likenesses to be violations of the Bible's admonition against graven images. Yet tourists snapped photo after photo of Amish people.

Jane enjoyed stopping at the stores and looking at the handmade furniture—dressers, rockers and cedar chests—and the homemade food stuffs—jams, jellies and pickled vegetables. However, she could do without all the novelty souvenirs—T-shirts, signs and posters.

After Sylvia purchased several handmade aprons at a country store and they had walked back to the car, Jane leaned against the door.

"Are you all right?" Sylvia asked.

"I think I've had enough," she said. "All the products are starting to blur together. I can't see one thing from another."

"I know what you mean." Sylvia lowered her voice. "After a while I feel like I am at the world's largest flea market."

"There are a lot of beautiful items, but it all just seems so…so…"

"Consumer driven?"

Jane nodded. "And exploitive. I feel sorry for the Amish. They have their name stamped on everything from food to T-shirts, some of which I'm sure they would not approve of."

Sylvia glanced at her watch. "It's a good time for a break, and it's also time for our lunch at Hannah's."

Back in the car, Sylvia directed Jane down a series of country lanes. They saw men plowing fields with horses and women hanging laundry on the line.

Jane felt as though their car was an intrusion. She suddenly felt out of place. "Sylvia, we don't have to have lunch here," she said.

"But we've been invited. Did you think I set up some sort of staged lunch?"

"Well..."

"You met Annie Stoltzfus. This is her mother, Hannah. She invited us to lunch because she knew I was bringing an English friend to Lancaster."

"English?" Jane asked.

"That is how the Amish refer to outsiders—non-Amish people," Sylvia said. "I've spoken to Hannah of you and Louise and Alice over the years, and she told me that if any of you were ever in her area, we should have lunch with her. So we arranged this."

"It's difficult to explain, but I feel out of place. Like I **don't** belong here."

"You're not like the usual tourist, trust me." Sylvia laid a hand on her arm. "This is a chance to meet a real family and see how they live."

"I feel like a snoop," Jane said.

"Well, you're not. You are an invited guest. And this is a wonderful opportunity to meet new people from a different culture. That's all," Sylvia said.

Jane let out a deep breath. "You're right. Thank you."

The Stoltzfus' farm looked similar to every other Amish farm they'd passed. From a distance, they could see the white clapboard house and what appeared to be a freshly painted white barn. Closer up, as they turned into the lane, they could see well-tended gardens.

Jane drove toward the yard.

"Park beside the buggy," Sylvia suggested.

Jane stopped the car and shut off the engine.

Shy children emerged from the field beside the house, from the barn and from the house itself. They hung back and observed the women in their yard.

Annie Stoltzfus bounded down the steps toward them. "Miss Songer! I'm so glad you and your friend could come for lunch. Hello, Miss Howard. Mam and I have been looking forward to this."

A woman appeared on the porch, and then approached

the Acorn Hill duo. "*Wilkum*," she said, smiling, gesturing for them to come inside.

All the curtains were made of white cotton and held up with two nails and a string, pulled taut. The dark wood floor was spotless and shining from varnish. The light blue walls were bare except for a general store calendar and a pair of cross-stitched Scripture verses.

Jane noticed that Hannah Stoltzfus had no buttons or zippers on her royal-blue dress or apron, only straight pins. The white cap on her head was heavily starched. Annie was dressed identically to her mother, as were the other girls who quietly poured into the room. The boys were dressed in blue shirts and black pants held up by suspenders. They smiled tentatively.

"It's good to see you, Hannah," Sylvia said, embracing her friend. "I'd like you to meet Jane Howard, one of the sisters I've told you about."

Hannah nodded at Jane. "It's good to meet you. A friend of Sylvia's is a friend of mine."

"Thank you, I feel the same way," Jane responded.

"The Howard sisters live in a very old home," Sylvia said.

"How old is your home?" Jane asked Hannah.

Hannah gestured around the room. "My husband's great-great-grandfather built this place when he was a young man."

"I don't believe ours is quite that old," Jane said, with a chuckle. "Grace Chapel Inn was built in the late nineteenth century."

Sylvia explained how the inn was their childhood home before the sisters had reunited to open a bed-and-breakfast.

"It's good for family to be together," Hannah said.

"Our aunt lives in the carriage house behind the main home," Jane said. "She's a widow, and her children live far away, so I think she enjoys living near family."

"We have an annex to our house called the *dawdi haus*, where my husband's parents lived until they passed on." Hannah paused. "I have been thinking about moving into the annex and letting my oldest son take over here."

"The Amish believe in caring for their elderly themselves. They don't rely on Social Security or retirement homes," Sylvia said.

"That's wonderful," Jane said. "I wish all families were like that."

Hannah looked slightly embarrassed at the praise and gestured toward the kitchen. "Lunch is ready, if you will come with me and have a seat."

In the kitchen, three long tables had been set up. Annie's younger brothers and sisters found their places at two of the tables. Hannah motioned her guests to the third, and she and Annie sat with them.

"First we will pray," Hannah said.

All the children bowed their heads, and the guests did the same. Hannah prayed for the nourishment of the food and thanked God for their guests' visit and asked for their safety on the return trip. Finally, she prayed for everyone's words to be good and true and for everyone, everywhere, to live in peace.

The second she finished the prayer, she and Annie were on their feet, bringing to the tables steaming bowls and platters of food. The meal began with a fruit salad, followed by golden, crisp fried chicken and a variety of vegetables and side dishes, including mounds of creamy mashed potatoes, homemade pickled beets, applesauce and fresh bread. After everyone was finished with the main course, Hannah served apple and shoofly pies.

As she finished her slice of the deliciously gooey molasses-and-brown-sugar shoofly pie, Jane resolved to ask Hannah for the recipe.

For the most part they ate in silence, and Jane noticed that the children were exceedingly well behaved. When the meal concluded and the children were excused, Annie turned to her mother. "Now, Mam? Please?"

A momentary frown crossed Hannah's face. She sighed and turned to Sylvia. "I'm sorry to speak in front of your friend, but I know you are returning soon."

"Yes, this afternoon," Sylvia said.

Hannah glanced at her daughter. "Annie, perhaps you had better go see about the young ones."

Annie nodded and left the room.

Hannah turned back to Sylvia. "My daughter is seventeen.

She is not yet baptized. Until she is, she is free to make her own choices about life." She turned to Jane and explained, "We allow our children a running-around time—*rumspringa*—to experience your world, the English world. It is difficult to do, but we parents turn our backs and allow our children a time of freedom."

"This is for Amish teenagers who are anywhere from sixteen to nineteen," Sylvia said to Jane. "Not everyone goes on a *rumspringa*, of course. Some already know that they want to be baptized and live the Amish life."

Hannah nodded. "But some desire to make as much mischief as possible. Annie is interested in a young man, Henry Byler, who seems intent on such. He has been racing buggies with other like-minded teenagers and smoking cigarettes and even"—she shuddered—"drinking beer at what they call 'hoedowns' out in the woods."

"You must be worried about Annie," Sylvia said, laying a hand over her friend's.

A tear trickled from Hannah's eye. She nodded. "My Annie is a good girl, but I'm afraid that she may be drawn to all this because of him. She hasn't participated in these activities—yet—but I feel it's only a matter of time."

"Is there anything we can do to help?" Jane asked.

Hannah looked at Sylvia. "Actually, there is something I want to ask you."

"Anything," Sylvia said.

Hannah drew a deep breath. "Annie is restless here, helping me to care for the younger ones. Perhaps if she could experience something new, a new place to live for a while. Even if it is not among the Amish, I could be happy if I knew she was safe. I feel certain that she will choose our life, but I don't want her to have any doubts."

"Would you like her to live with me for a while?" Sylvia asked. "She could live in my home and work at my store."

"It's asking a lot of you."

"Nonsense," Sylvia said. "It would be fun for me to have the company and to have such a good seamstress help me at the shop."

"My sisters and I could help to keep an eye on her," Jane said. "She would be welcome at Grace Chapel Inn any time."

"Perhaps she could do some work for you there as well," Hannah said. "I don't want her to be idle."

"Well, we wouldn't use her as free labor," Jane said, "but if she's interested in earning some spending money, we could find some things for her to do."

Hannah looked relieved. "If her hands are busy at a useful enterprise, she won't have time to get into trouble."

"Jane and I need to return to Acorn Hill this afternoon," Sylvia said. "She and her sisters have guests arriving soon. How about if we give you some time for Annie to get her things together and for you to break the news to her brothers and sisters? We can return later today to pick her up."

"I think that would be best. Thank you." Hannah's eyes were wet with tears. "I know she has wanted something beyond this farm for a while. It would be good for her to get away from Henry Byler. I want her to experience life with other young people her age, even if they are English. I would be unhappy if she didn't choose the Amish way of life, but I would not die. I want her to make the choice for herself." She stood. "But it would mean so much to me to know that she is being watched over."

"I promise that I will do that," Sylvia said.

"So do I." Jane nodded her agreement.

Jane and Sylvia soberly finished the rest of their sightseeing excursion. Their hearts saddened for Hannah, they didn't have much enthusiasm for more touring. They did stop by Elijah Hoppenstedt's pretzel store in Lancaster. Though they were full from Hannah's lunch, the sight of the freshly baked, twisted and salted pretzels was tempting. They bought some to take home.

After that, they rode back to Fenella's. They packed their bags and thanked Fenella for a lovely stay.

"You ladies have a safe trip back," Fenella said, giving

them each a warm hug. "Usually when I meet folks, they're visiting from big cities and I say something like, 'Don't forget us here in the country.' But I believe Acorn Hill is smaller than Lancaster, so I'll just say, 'Don't forget us.'"

"Thank you, Fenella," Jane said. "I don't believe I could."

They rode to Hannah's home, where Annie waited on the porch steps. She was still wearing her Amish dress, but she had removed the apron and cap. When she saw Sylvia and Jane, she jumped up and called into the house, "Mam! They're here!"

Jane and Sylvia got out of the car, and Hannah Stoltzfus appeared on the front porch, wiping her hands on her apron. She looked as though she was about to cry, but she smiled at the two women. She gave Annie a brief hug and kissed her on the forehead. "Take care," was all she said.

Annie nodded solemnly, then turned to Jane and Sylvia with sparkling eyes. "I'm ready."

"Do you have a bag?" Jane asked.

Annie shook her head, then held up a small drawstring cloth sack that Jane hadn't even noticed. "Just this."

Hannah's face reddened. "I should give you some money for clothes. I'm sure she'll want some English ones."

"Don't worry about it," Sylvia said softly. "It will be my gift to Annie."

Hannah wrung her hands in her apron. "I have heard

that some of today's fashion for girls are not ... appropriate. Short shirts, skirts ..." She blinked.

"I'll make sure that she chooses appropriate attire," Sylvia said.

Annie hopped into the back of the car, sitting forward on the seat until Jane reminded her to buckle her seatbelt. Annie sheepishly complied. "I've ridden in an automobile before. Once when I broke my arm and had to go to the hospital, and another time when one of the younger ones was sick."

Hannah waved once, then retreated into the house.

Annie waved at her remaining brothers and sisters, who stayed on the porch. When Jane turned onto the country road, Annie sighed with excitement. "I can't believe Mam let me go with you, Miss Songer."

"She loves you very much," Sylvia said.

For the return trip to Acorn Hill. Jane and Sylvia were more silent than on their journey out. Annie, however, could barely contain herself. She waved at people they passed on the road, even those she didn't know. As the county faded behind them, she hummed tunelessly, like a child. Jane found herself smiling. Annie *was* still a child in many ways, and life had suddenly become one grand adventure. Though Jane doubted that she was thinking about it at the moment, Annie would have to make up her mind about her future life with or without the Amish.

Jane prayed that she, Sylvia and everyone else that Annie met in Acorn Hill would make the girl feel welcome. She prayed that God would make Annie's decision clear as soon as possible. Hannah's sad face and reluctant good-bye wave were fresh in Jane's memory.

Chapter Four

*T*he sisters were expecting guests Friday, so when Jane arrived home Thursday afternoon, she began to make her plans for breakfasts.

"It'd be nice to bake something new," she said to Louise as she pored over an Amish cookbook she'd purchased in Lancaster. "The food I ate the past few days was wonderful."

"I'm sure that it was nothing more than what you cook, Jane," Louise said. "Or could cook."

"Thanks, Louise." Jane shook her head. "I have a feeling there's something I'm supposed to be doing today, but I can't think of what it is."

"Is it something to do with the ice-cream social tonight at Grace Chapel? Didn't you promise to bake something?" Louise asked.

"That's it! Thank you. I promised Pastor Ken and Pastor Henry that I would bring a cake or two for the dessert table. I'd better get to work."

Grace Chapel was the church next door to Grace Chapel Inn. The Howard sisters' father, Daniel Howard, had been the pastor at Grace Chapel for many years. After his death, when the sisters had reunited and decided to open their home as a bed-and-breakfast, they agreed that the inn should reflect the church's name.

"Pastor Ken" was Rev. Kenneth Thompson, Grace Chapel's minister. A childless widower, he had grown up in Boston and started his pastoral career there. Some time after his wife's death, he decided to move to Acorn Hill and to Grace Chapel.

"Pastor Henry" was Rev. Henry Ley, the associate pastor and also a member of the church board. His wife Patsy had suggested that Grace Chapel hold an ice-cream social for its members as a way of welcoming spring.

In the evening, with the inn ready for the next day's guests, the sisters headed to the Grace Chapel get-together. The lawn area designated for the event was already filling with members of all ages. A table with cakes and assorted goodies was set to one side. Another table held several punch bowls of pink and yellow lemonade.

Each dressed in a turn-of-the-century costume, Patsy Ley arranged the last of the folding chairs, while Henry Ley cranked the handle of an old-fashioned ice-cream maker.

"Oh, look at those big sleeves and that flowing skirt on Patsy's dress," Jane said. "She looks lovely."

"And that high, stiff collar, vest and coat of Henry's," Alice said. She and Jane approached Henry Ley, who was working hard at the crank next to the cake table. "You look wonderful—like you two just stepped out of the early twentieth century."

"Th-that's just what we were trying to imitate," Henry said, smiling as he continued to turn the handle on the machine. "The 1904 World's Fair in St. Louis was where the ice-cream cone was invented. An ice-cream seller ran out of dishes, and the waffle vendor in the next booth came up with the idea of scooping ice cream into a rolled-up waffle. We don't have any waffles t-tonight, but those cakes sure look g-good." He paused from cranking to run a finger between his collar and neck. "Maybe it wasn't s-such a good idea to wear these clothes on such a hot day."

"It is a little warm for those heavy clothes," Jane said, "but you and Patsy do look the part for an old-fashioned ice-cream social. Why don't you get some lemonade from Aunt Ethel? I see she's manning the punch bowl over there. Get a glass and find yourself a shady spot to rest. I'll work this thing for a while."

"Well…"

Jane gently moved between Henry and the ice-cream machine and started cranking. "See? No problem. I'll work for a while, then someone else will relieve me."

Alice set the chocolate cake she was holding on the table. "I'll walk over there with you, Henry. I want to say hello to Aunt Ethel."

Louise set down the other of Jane's chocolate cakes. "Looks like your cakes are in good company, Jane. Here's a peach cobbler, a pound cake, an apple pie ..."

"Good. I love a selection of desserts." Jane stopped to pant with exertion. "Boy, this is hard work."

Louise smiled as she spotted Kenneth Thompson approaching. Tall, lean and dressed in neatly pressed chino slacks and a light-green polo shirt, he looked more like a golf pro than a man of the cloth. He smiled at them. "Hello, Pastor Ken," Louise said.

"Hi, Louise. Jane, let me help you with the cranking." He moved behind the freezer to take over for Jane. She willingly gave up her place, shaking her hand to loosen the tense muscles.

"*Whew*. Thank you. That's harder than it looks," she said.

She watched him for a moment. He smiled, his hazel eyes twinkling. "What?"

"*You* don't seem to be having any trouble."

He shrugged. "Must be all those years of college baseball I played. Lots of catching and pitching really built up the strength in my arm." He winked. "Or maybe it's from pounding the pulpit every Sunday."

Louise and Jane laughed. It was difficult to imagine the gentle, kind pastor as a fire-and-brimstone type.

"How was your trip to the Amish country?" he asked

Jane over the noise of the machine. "Did you find any good antiques?"

"We saw quite a few but weren't tempted to buy," Jane said. "I'm sure you would have found some of the shops interesting, since antiques are your forte." Jane was referring to his having grown up helping his parents in their antique store. She went on to tell him about Annie Stoltzfus coming to live with Sylvia, and that the two had passed up the social in order to shop for Annie's clothes.

Pastor Ken listened attentively. "The Amish are an interesting people. Do you think Annie will want to attend Grace Chapel with Sylvia?" he asked.

"I never thought about that," Jane said. "I wonder if her mother would be upset if she did."

"It sounds as though her mother is giving the girl free rein spiritually. I think that's wise. No one should be forced to join a church—any church. God gave us free will."

"I imagine Sylvia will leave it up to Annie," Jane said.

"Which is also wise," Pastor Ken said. "Say, how long am I supposed to crank this thing anyway?"

Louise looked at Jane, who laughed. "I have no idea. Henry didn't tell us."

"Maybe you'd better find him," Rev. Thompson said. "I think my arm's starting to seize up. I'd hate to have to go on the DL."

"DL?" Louise asked.

"Disabled list, sorry. It's a baseball term for a player who has an injury and can't play. That allows the team to bring up another player from the minor leagues."

"Oh," said Louise, perplexed. "I never learned much of anything about baseball other than 'three strikes and you're out.'"

Rev. Thompson laughed. "And that's a good bit of the game."

"We'll go find Henry," Jane said. I think I see him over there. Say, Pastor Ken. Why aren't you in costume like Henry and Patsy?"

"What? In this weather?"

Though the ice-cream social had been promoted as a come-and-go event, it seemed as though everyone showed up at the same time. Jane and Louise found themselves cutting slices of cake and spooning cobbler into bowls, while Alice manned the ice-cream scooper. When someone relieved the sisters of their duties and they took their turns waiting in line, they learned that the hand-cranked ice cream was tutti-frutti. Another freezer held vanilla bean, and still another, strawberry. Lloyd Tynan's secretary, Bella Paoli, brought a freezer of chocolate, which she had made at home. A fifty-something blonde, she had a notorious sweet tooth, yet she managed to retain a youthful, slim figure.

The Howard sisters found folding chairs together with Rev. Thompson, Rev. Lee and Patsy, Lloyd and Ethel, and Bella and Hank Young. Hank was Acorn Hill's resident computer geek and had recently graduated from college. He designed Web sites and did other freelance computer repair and programming work.

They all sat in a congenial circle, scooping the creamy, cold confection from bowls, which also held their choices of baked dessert.

"*Mmm*," Jane said, savoring each bite of strawberry ice cream and pound cake. "Eating ice cream in warm weather reminds me of being a kid, sitting on the back porch with my bare feet dangling off the side, watching the fireflies."

"My father used to make ice cream at least once a month during the heat of the summer," Lloyd said. "This reminds me of that."

"It's not the heat of the summer, but it is rather warm for May," Louise said. She swatted at a bug. "Please don't tell me that was a mosquito. It's too early for swarming insects."

Everyone laughed.

"The warm weather reminds me of baseball," Rev. Thompson said. "Dusting off the bases, mowing a grassy field and chalking lines for the runners." He sighed. "At least that's what *I* remember about being a kid in warm weather."

"Me, too, now that you mention it," Lloyd said, "although when I was growing up, we usually used a pasture."

"I never played, of course," Ethel said, "but I remember watching the boys play. If I ever wanted to participate in a sport, I think it would have been baseball. There's something simple and wholly American about the game."

"Ah, to be a child again," Jane said thoughtfully. "Things become so much more complicated when you grow up."

"Speaking of growing up and baseball," Bella said, nodding at Rev. Thompson, "I hear that the Little League team needs a coach this year."

"What happened to Gerald Morton?" Lloyd asked. "He's coached the local team for the last five years."

"He has a slipped disk," Bella said.

"Ah. He's on the DL," Louise said, raising her eyebrow and nodding at Rev. Thompson. "I wonder who they'll bring up from the minor leagues to replace him."

Rev. Thompson laughed, appreciating not only her improved baseball knowledge, but her sense of humor as well.

The others didn't catch the exchange.

"Nobody's offered to step in for Gerald," Bella continued. "If someone doesn't volunteer soon, there won't be a team this year."

"No baseball in Acorn Hill?" Lloyd thundered in his best politician's voice. "Why, it's a disaster!"

Jane nudged Rev. Thompson. "You could coach them," she whispered.

He smiled. "Jane, I hardly think it's appropriate for a pastor to—"

"To *what?*" she asked, with a playful challenge in her voice. "To help out some needy kids? What if you hadn't had a coach when you were growing up? After all, Jesus said, 'Do unto others as you would have them—'"

He held up his hands in mock surrender. "All right! If they'll have me, I'll be delighted to coach."

Lloyd perked up. "*You're* volunteering for the job, Pastor?"

Rev. Thompson's eyes twinkled. "I believe I've been volunteered. Don't you think I'm up to it?"

"No, no, no, it's not that," Lloyd said. "I just thought that, well, what with your schedule and all and who knows what you might be needed for…"

Hank Young raised his hand. "If Pastor Ken coaches, then I volunteer to help him. I can pick up the slack."

Everyone stared.

"You're interested in baseball?" Jane asked.

"I'm not a big Red Sox fan, like Pastor Ken," he said, "but I've followed the game since I was a kid. I don't park myself behind a computer 24-7, you know."

"Although I understand fans can watch games on the Internet now," Rev. Thompson said, smiling.

"That's right," Hank said, obviously not minding the ribbing. "I use it sometimes to keep up with my favorite teams. The truth is, I always wanted to play baseball on a team, but the Little League in our area had some serious players, and I just wasn't up to their level. In high school, I was the team trainer."

"So you know the game well?" Lloyd asked.

Hank nodded. "I've practically memorized *The Baseball Encyclopedia*."

"I doubt that these kids need to know player statistics or history like Tinker to Evers to Chance," Bella said.

Hank stared at her. "How do you know about that?"

"They played for the Chicago Cubs during the early twentieth century and revolutionized the double play," she said. "Every hard-core baseball fan knows about them."

"I didn't realize you were such an enthusiast," Hank said.

Bella shrugged. "I used to play ball a little when I was a kid, and after I left home I made a study of the game."

"Do you have a favorite team?" Hank asked.

Bella shot Rev. Thompson a sideways glance. "The Yankees."

Hank laughed. "I'm guessing that you and Pastor Ken have had this conversation before."

"What am I missing?" Louise whispered to Jane.

"The Boston Red Sox—Pastor Ken's favorite team—are the biggest rivals of the New York Yankees," she whispered back.

"Pastor Ken and I have reached an agreement to disagree," Bella said pleasantly.

"Well, now that the matter of the Little League team is settled," Lloyd said, slapping his knees. "I'd like to hear about your trip to the Amish country, Jane."

Jane detailed the trip and told them about Annie Stoltzfus. "She'll be living with Sylvia indefinitely," she said, then explained about *rumspringa*.

"Maybe she'd like to talk to some of our school-age kids. It'd be a real cultural treat for them," Lloyd said.

Bella, who had looked thoughtful during the talk about Annie, said, "Someone should mention it to Vera Humbert. I'm sure she and her fifth-grade class would be interested, and they're at the age where they could ask good questions."

"What will Annie do about school?" Lloyd asked.

"The Amish only attend through eighth grade," Jane explained, "so Annie is finished with her education, as far as her family is concerned."

She shook her head, then continued. "I agree with much of their simple way of living, but I wonder about stopping school at eighth grade. When I was in high school, I could have done without chemistry and physics, for example, but now I'm glad I got an introduction to them."

"I feel the same way," Louise said.

"I wonder how the Amish feel about not raising any future doctors or nurses," Jane said, glancing at Alice.

"I wondered about that too," Alice said.

"They don't feel that everyone must live the way they do," Bella said. "They only choose for themselves."

"It's certainly intriguing to think about how they manage to live in a world that doesn't share their belief system," Jane said. "I don't know how they manage it."

Ethel sighed. "This conversation is getting too deep for me. All I know is that the Amish consider themselves different, and they certainly act like it. It will be interesting to see how Annie adjusts to Acorn Hill."

"Indeed," Louise said.

Lloyd coughed. "Being here with all of you reminds me of some business that I want to discuss. Hank?"

The young man hastily swallowed a spoonful of ice cream and chocolate cake. "Yes, sir?"

"Is there any chance you'd have time to help develop a Web site for Acorn Hill?"

"Why of course," Hank said, surprise registering on his face. "I didn't realize you were interested in getting Acorn Hill online."

"It occurred to me the other day that our library is online, but the town isn't. I think you looked up information about Lancaster County before you traveled, didn't you, Jane? Well, I'd like to have a place where potential visitors could find information about Acorn Hill and links to attractions in our area."

"That's a wonderful idea," Jane said. "I'm sure a lot of the shops in town would like to be featured on their own page too. I bet Craig Tracy would want Wild Things to have a page where he could show floral designs and such, and I'm sure Sylvia would want Sylvia's Buttons on a page too."

"And Fred Humbert would probably like a link to his hardware store," Louise said.

"And Wilhelm Wood for Time for Tea," Jane added.

"And—"

Lloyd held up his hands to stop further speculation. "I'm glad we're all in agreement that this is a good idea. Are you willing to take on the job, Hank? Acorn Hill would pay your standard rate, of course."

"Sure, I'll do it. I'd be glad to give the town a discount, though," he said, then glanced around the group. "I'd be willing to share the work if someone wants to help me. There will be a lot of information to compile."

"I'll help," Bella said. "As Lloyd's assistant, that would make the most sense. I'm already on the city clock," she said, winking. "Lloyd and I can brainstorm, and I can act as liaison for town members. I'll give you the information, Hank, and you can work your Web-page magic."

"Great. Bella, why don't you and Lloyd decide what's needed and wanted, then give me a call? I'm between projects right now, so I'm free most days, *er*, except for Little League practices, that is," he said, glancing at Rev. Thompson. "I almost forgot my other new responsibility. Anyway, I'll get an ISP and register a domain name."

Lloyd shook his head. "I have no idea what you just said, but I'll leave it in your and Bella's capable hands. I know you'll do Acorn Hill proud."

"Same goes for the Little League team," Rev. Thompson said.

Hank beamed with the praise. "I was wondering what I'd do with myself in the weeks ahead, and now it looks like I have plenty to keep me busy. Thanks for the vote of confidence, everybody. I'm looking forward to all the fun."

The sisters helped to clean up after the social and then returned to the inn.

"*Whew*," Jane said, sinking into a kitchen chair. "That was so nice."

"I agree. It's pleasant to be outdoors this early," Alice said. "During recent Mays, we've had some pretty cold weather."

"Not this year," Louise said. "I just hope it is not an indication of a particularly hot summer. It's comfortable now, but I hate to think of the temperature increasing correspondingly when we are moving into July and August. I find it difficult to get motivated when it's hot outside."

"Speaking of motivated," Alice said. "I've been thinking

about something Aunt Ethel said right before you left for Lancaster, Jane."

"What was it, Alice?" Jane asked.

"She told me that she felt bored. In a rut," Alice said. "I was just wondering if she was over those feelings. She seemed quieter than usual tonight."

"I did notice that she seemed less animated," Louise said. "Normally she's right in the thick of conversation, but she was fairly withdrawn."

"That's just because the conversation was about Web sites and baseball," Jane said. "Two things that she knows little about. Anyway, I thought she seemed fine."

"Well, if she is bored, I feel sorry for her," Louise said. "I know it is difficult for you to understand, Jane, because you are such an active person."

"And have a multitude of interests," Alice added.

Louise nodded. "But when you get older, into your seventies or eighties, it's harder to try new things."

"What do you suggest we do for her?" Jane asked.

Louise shook her head. "I can't think of anything offhand, but we should keep our eyes open for possibilities. I'd suggest she help Hank, but Bella volunteered for the job."

"It's probably just as well," Jane said. "The Web site team needs someone with good business sense, and let's face it: Aunt Ethel is more of a people person than a facts-and-figures type."

"*Hmm*. That is a good point," Louise said. "Whatever task we find for Aunt Ethel should be people-oriented. Is there any volunteer work to be had at the Potterston Hospital, Alice?"

Alice shook her head. "They don't need anyone right now. I spoke with the director of volunteer services just the other day to tell her that we have too many volunteers in some parts of the hospital. They're practically tripping over each other."

"I wonder if Vera needs help in her classroom," Louise said.

"She has a parent helping as a teacher's aide, I believe," Alice said.

Louise sighed. "We'll just have to keep looking. Meanwhile, I'd better do one last check on the guest rooms."

"Do you know anything about our new guests?" Jane asked.

Louise shook her head. "Not much. They are a family of five from the Northeast—the Campanellas—that's all I know."

Chapter Five

The next morning the sisters went about their normal routine. Alice had to work at Potterston Hospital, but she promised that she'd be home in time to greet their guests. Louise had an adult student for a morning piano lesson, and Jane took advantage of not having guests and ate breakfast at the Coffee Shop.

"Thank you, Hope," Jane said as the waitress poured her another cup of coffee. "It always feels luxurious to be waited on."

Hope Collins was a woman in her thirties who had worked at the Coffee Shop for a long time. "I know you must like an occasional break from preparing those elaborate breakfasts," she said, setting down the coffee carafe.

"Well, they're not necessarily elaborate, but they are substantial. Like this French toast, which was delicious. Give my compliments to the cook. And to June," Jane said, referring to June Carter, the Coffee Shop's owner.

"The bread was from the Good Apple Bakery," Hope said. "Most folks can't tell the difference in bread—particularly with French toast—but I'm sure you can."

Jane nodded as she finished the last bite with a satisfied sigh. She dabbed her mouth with her napkin and asked, "So life's treating you all right?"

"I suppose so," Hope said. She glanced back at the kitchen and, not seeing her employer, sat down across from Jane. "Did you hear that Nia is going to be out of town for a week?"

Nia Komonos was Acorn Hill's librarian.

"Everything's all right, I hope," Jane said.

Hope nodded. "All I know is that she's going out of town and leaving her assistant in charge."

"That's quite a responsibility for Malinda," Jane said.

Malinda Mitschke was a graduate student in library science at Drexel University in Philadelphia. An Acorn Hill native, she commuted to the university to attend classes.

"I don't know if the girl's up to it," Hope said. "I've known her ever since I've lived in Acorn Hill, of course. She doesn't seem to be the take-charge type, if you know what I mean. She's more of a bookworm than a leader."

"I'm sure she'll do fine," Jane said, wanting Hope to give the girl a chance.

"Hope?" a voice called from the kitchen.

"Oops, that's June." Hope scrambled to her feet, grabbing the carafe. "You want any more coffee before I go?"

"No, thanks. Just my check when you get a minute."

"Got it right here." Hope fished a receipt from the pocket of her apron. "Have a good day."

"Same to you," Jane said as the waitress scurried off.

After breakfast, Jane decided to take a short walking tour of her hometown. When she'd moved back home from San Francisco after her father's death, her initial take on Acorn Hill was that time seemed to drag there and attitudes were, well, provincial. Now the town was home again, and she no longer felt that she had to change herself to fit in. She was a part of it now, and she reveled in the slower pace and in the warm friendliness of its citizens. As she walked, she thought of all her many close friends and acquaintances.

She found herself smiling. It was true that she sometimes missed the fine dining and multitude of attractions of northern California in general and San Francisco in particular. But Acorn Hill had charms of its own: a close-knit attitude among its citizens but an open-arms policy for visitors. The rest of the world was certainly accessible enough through planes, cars and the information superhighway, but as she waved to various residents and shopkeepers along her way, she acknowledged that Acorn Hill was definitely the place she wanted to be now.

On impulse, she turned right off Hill Street and headed down Acorn Avenue toward the library. Jane admired Nia Komonos. The library had a small budget, but Nia managed to use every penny thriftily and to the town's best advantage.

Inside the building, famous authors looked down at Jane from their posters on the library's walls. In the center of the main room, a square glass case contained items that related to the monthly theme. This month, Nia had arranged an artful tribute to spring, complete with artificial branches of dogwood and sprigs of mountain laurel, Pennsylvania's state flower. There was even a realistic toy rabbit tucked whimsically into the corner of the case.

The three computers with Internet access were occupied, and only one of the library's armchairs was available. Patrons browsed the DVD and video lending collections, probably in anticipation of the weekend. The children's section was filled with tots sitting cross-legged on the carpeted floor, trying their best to sit still while a library volunteer read.

A volunteer clerk stamped books at the checkout desk, smiling at Jane as she walked toward the administrative office. Normally Nia was somewhere in the book stacks or visible in the main part of the library. Jane didn't see her in either place, so she assumed Nia was in her office.

The office door was open. Nia and Malinda sat side by side, going over a worksheet. Nia glanced up. "Hello, Jane. What can I do for you?"

"I just came by to say hello. I didn't mean to interrupt."

"I think we're ready for a break," Nia said with a laugh.

Malinda nodded, looking relieved. "I'll see how story time is going in the children's section."

"Thanks, Malinda," Nia said, smiling as her assistant headed back into the library. "What brings you here, Jane?"

"Gossip, I suppose," she said.

Nia smiled. "You must have been at the Coffee Shop this morning, huh?"

"Well . . ."

"It's all right. I knew Hope would tell at least one person. I stopped in for a cup of java this morning, and I told her about my trip. Is that why you're here?"

"I just wanted to make sure everything was okay with you. It is a little unusual to have the librarian leave for a week."

Nia laughed. "Let me put your mind at rest. I'm going to a librarians' conference in Pittsburgh."

"Oh, that's all. I really was a bit worried," Jane said.

"Well . . ." Nia's eyes began to sparkle. "I've mentioned that I have a boyfriend in Pittsburgh, right?"

"Yes."

Her smile widened. "Oh, Jane, I shouldn't tell anybody, but I'm just so excited. I think this might be it."

"You think he might pop the question?"

Nia nodded. "At least I think we're going to talk about the possibility of getting married."

"That's wonderful!"

"Yes, but—"

"Whoa! 'Yes, but'?"

Nia sighed. "He really likes his job, and he likes working

in Pittsburgh. Even if he wanted to move, it'd be difficult for him to find work in this area. Marriage would mean that I'd probably have to leave Acorn Hill and move back home to Pittsburgh."

"*Ohhh*," Jane whispered.

"I love it here. So you see my dilemma."

"Have you said anything to anybody else about this possibility?"

Nia shook her head. "I wanted to see how this week goes. It may be that Marco doesn't intend to propose at all. I may be reading too much into our relationship, such as it is." She sighed. "It *is* difficult trying to get together, with my living in one end of the state and his being in the other."

Jane touched her friend's arm. "It will work out, Nia. One way or another, it'll be clear to you. I'll pray that it is."

Nia leaned back in her chair. "Thanks, Jane. In the meantime, would you please keep this to yourself? I don't want anyone else to know. No sense in alarming people, and the fewer who know, the fewer explanations I'll have to offer. The good thing is that my trip will give Malinda a chance to handle things on her own."

"Do you think she's ready for it?" Jane asked. "I don't mean to be critical, but . . ."

"I know she can be timid, but I think being thrust into a position of leadership will teach her to stand on her own two **feet**. At least I hope so."

Jane walked back through town, stopping to purchase flowers at Wild Things from Craig Tracy. He was busy with another customer, so she went to the cooler and selected several peonies and irises and set them on the counter for Craig to wrap. While she waited for him, she studied packets of seeds he had for sale by the checkout area.

When the other customer left, Craig turned to her with a smile and began arranging her flowers on a sheet of green, waxy florist paper. "Is there anything else I can get for you, Jane?"

She replaced the packets and sighed. "I probably shouldn't buy these just yet. There might be a late frost."

Craig propped his elbows on the counter. "You are just like the rest of my customers. They're all chomping at the bit to put their gardens in."

"I think I'm a little more eager than usual because of my trip to Lancaster County."

She told him about seeing Rebecca King working in her garden. "I don't know, Craig," she said, finishing the tale. "Someone like that is so much more in touch with the earth and with gardening. I feel like a dilettante next to someone who depends on her vegetable garden for her food. Does that seem odd?"

"No, but you are certainly not a dilettante. I think it's helpful to view gardening in another light. I think we value our own gardens more when we see how much someone else depends on hers."

Jane studied the seeds again and chose several packets. "Add these to the flowers, please. I think I'm going to go home and work in my garden."

Jane hugged the flowers and seed packets close as she headed home. She could envision tilling the earth, planting the seeds, watching them grow.

As she passed Grace Chapel, Rev. Thompson waved to her. He was dressed in a Red Sox cap, polo shirt, shorts and cross trainers.

"I was afraid I missed you when I didn't find you at the inn," he said.

"Have the Red Sox drafted you?" she asked, smiling.

"No, but I'm on my way to my first Little League meeting with Hank."

"That's great. I know you'll both do a fine job."

"I was wondering . . ." He hesitated. "I know it's a lot to ask . . ."

"What?"

"I was wondering if you'd consider helping Hank and me out a bit too. We could really use another person. Just when you have time, that is. But I'm the coach, and Hank wants to work with the pitchers. It would just be good to have someone else checking on the kids while they do their drills or while they're taking BP."

"Uh, BP?"

"Sorry. Batting practice."

Jane smiled. "Pastor Ken, I don't know the baseball lingo. I barely know the rules."

He squinted into the sun. "I know you're busy. I just thought it might be good for them to see a woman helping out, particularly since no girls signed up for the team."

"Really?" Jane shifted her bags to the other hand. "I guess I could attend a practice, maybe, just to see how things are, of course."

"Of course," he said solemnly. "I understand you have guests arriving today, so it's probably not a good time now. But Hank and I are meeting with the kids tomorrow morning at ten o'clock, if you can make it."

"I'll see what I can do."

"Thanks, Jane."

She headed up the path to Grace Chapel Inn, shaking her head. What had she gotten herself into?

"There you are," Louise said, greeting her at the door. "Our guests have just arrived. They're in the library with Alice."

Jane thought guiltily about the flowers, which should have already been arranged and in place for the guests' arrival. Alice had worked her shift at the hospital and yet *she* managed to be home in time. "I'm sorry I'm late. I had an interesting morning."

"You'll have to tell me about it later," Louise said, relieving Jane of her purchases. "I'll take these to the kitchen. Go say hello to our guests."

"Sure thing. Oh, and stick the flowers in water, would you please? I'll arrange them later."

Now that her hands were free, she smoothed her hair and straightened her black T-shirt and tan slacks. She opened the door and entered the library, a smile on her face. "Hi. I'm Jane Howard."

A man, a woman and three teenage girls smiled back. The man rose from his seat on a wing chair and held out his hand. Like his wife and daughters, he was blond, tanned and fit and had a dazzling white smile. "Hello, Jane. I'm Vaughn Campanella, and this is my wife Allison. These are our daughters, Lauren, Sidney and Marsha."

"It's nice to meet you." Jane shook his hand.

Allison also rose and moved toward Jane to shake her hand. "We've already heard so much about you. You're the chef, gardener, all-around Martha Stewart."

Jane laughed. "Well, you know all about me, but I know very little about you. I heard that a family from the Northeast was coming to stay with us for two weeks, but that's all. Aren't you girls supposed to be in school?"

"But we *are*," Lauren, who appeared to be the eldest of the girls, said. "We live in Rhode Island, and we're actually in school here studying design—boat design."

Allison laughed. "You look perplexed, Jane. Yes, my daughters are still teenagers. Lauren is seventeen, Sidney is sixteen and Marsha is fifteen. We homeschool, and the girls had an interest in studying boats and ships. We've been studying the history of shipbuilding, among other things."

"Which led into a study of ship and boat design," Vaughn said.

"Then we heard about the cardboard-boat regatta."

Jane smiled. "Oh yes, the annual charity event in Riverton. I've heard it's lots of fun, but I've never attended. How does it work?"

"Contestants build boats out of cardboard in advance of the event, then race the boats against each other in a body of water, in this case, an Olympic-size swimming pool," Vaughn said. "They also have another competition in which contestants build their boats on site, then race them."

"We're going to build our boat in advance," Lauren said proudly. "We've already been working on our design."

"These are small boats, like paper boats?" Jane asked.

The Campanellas laughed. "Oh no," Marsha said. "They're big enough for three to five people to sit in and row. They're like canoes."

"You're going to build a canoe here? At Grace Chapel Inn?" Jane asked.

Alice, who had been sitting quietly listening to all of this, hastily said, "They'll work on it outside, of course. I suggested that they could store it at night on the rear porch. I think that should be just enough space, given the size of the boat they plan to build."

Louise entered the room and stood beside Jane. "You've heard about the boat regatta?"

"Yes, and it sounds like loads of fun." Jane turned to the Campanellas. "You're welcome to store any paint or other construction items in the garden shed."

"Thanks," Vaughn said. "Say, you ladies should plan to attend the regatta. It's for a good cause, after all, with the entry fees and the profits from concessions going to the local nature center."

"Everyone just has a fun, crazy time," Allison said. "You wouldn't believe some of the boats people build and the costumes they wear. Last year, at a regatta near home, a bunch of men dressed up like past presidents, complete with suits and masks. Another group built cube-shaped boats and painted them white with black dots to resemble dice. They dressed up like gamblers from *Guys and Dolls*."

"There are official timekeepers who decide who's won the races," Vaughn added. "And there are judges who pick 'best of show,' 'best *Titanic* sink' and things like that."

"It really does sound like fun," Alice said.

"Say, Alice, would your ANGELs like to participate?" Jane asked, referring to the group of girls that Alice taught at Grace Chapel on Wednesday nights.

"I don't know if they'd be interested," Alice said. "But I'll ask them. Now that you mention it, the challenge might be good for us."

Chapter Six

The Campanellas had paid for two rooms. Since there were no other guests scheduled during their stay, Louise told them that they could have their pick of the four guest rooms.

Jane excused herself, and Louise and Alice took the family upstairs to the second floor. After investigating the accommodations, the delighted family stood in the hallway to discuss which rooms they should take. The daughters agreed that Lauren, as the oldest, should pick which room the girls would share. She chose the Sunrise Room, falling in love with its pale-blue ragged-paint walls and accents of white and yellow, along with the patchwork quilt of matching colors.

It didn't take Allison and Vaughn long to decide which room to choose for their own, either. "I like the one you call the Sunset Room," Allison said. "The walls are just the shade of a perfect sunset, and the antiqued furniture and Impressionist prints make me feel right at home. One of my hobbies is painting."

"I'm choosing the Sunrise Room," Lauren said, "but I like the Symphony Room, too, because of its name." She turned toward Louise. "I'd love to play the piano in the parlor. I know that you give lessons here, but if you're not using the piano in the parlor, may I play it?"

"By all means," Louise said. "I would be delighted. It's always nice to meet a fellow pianist."

Lauren beamed. "I'm thinking about studying music in college. Do you have any recommendations?"

"Well, I earned my degree at the conservatory in Philadelphia. My late husband taught there as well. We both thought it was a wonderful school. You might consider looking into it."

"We'll add it to our list of schools to investigate," Vaughn said. "We were hoping for something close to Rhode Island, but Philadelphia isn't that far away."

"Maybe we could even visit the conservatory while we're here," Allison said. She smiled at Alice and Louise. "That's one of the beauties of homeschooling. You can set your own schedule and don't have to work around school vacations."

"And I work at home, so that's even more convenient," Vaughn said. "We like to travel as much as possible, my schedule permitting."

"What do you do for a living?" Alice asked.

"I'm a financial analyst. I'm taking a vacation these two weeks."

"Before we had kids, I worked with him in the same office," Allison said. She slipped her arm around Vaughn's waist and smiled. "In fact, that's where we met. Now he's self-employed."

Louise leaned forward, curious. "Do you have to make accommodations with your local school authorities?"

"Homeschooling is legal all across America," Allison said. "Each state has different rules, though. In Rhode Island, the students' attendance must be roughly the same as those attending public schools, and certain subjects such as reading, writing, American history and arithmetic must be taught. The home school is subject to an annual assessment."

Louise was intrigued. "How do you know that the girls are getting the information that they need? Do you give them a standardized test each year?"

"Occasionally we test them to see if they're on a par with their age level," Vaughn said. "So far, they've always scored at least a grade or two ahead."

"Do you miss being around other kids your own age?" Alice asked.

"We're around people of all ages," Marsha said. "That's what I like best about homeschooling. My friends who go to public school are stuck all day with kids their own age."

"We're around younger kids, older kids, adults, and yes, kids our age," Lauren said.

Alice smiled. "I think it sounds wonderful. If you need any extra space for your studies, don't hesitate to ask."

"Thank you," Allison said. "We might just take advantage

of your library or parlor occasionally. We'll be concentrating on boatbuilding while we're here—this is a learning vacation of sorts. But we'll still need some space to spread out with papers and books to do math."

"We insist on keeping up with math," Vaughn said, placing his hands on Marsha's shoulders.

"Dad knows it's my least favorite subject," she said, smiling up at her father.

"I know, but it's important to master."

Allison smiled at her daughters. "Why don't we put our suitcases away and walk around for a bit? The distance to town seemed walkable."

"Yes, it's a comfortable walk," Alice said. "Louise and I will leave you alone to settle in. When you're ready for your walk, let one of us know. We'll point you in the right direction and tell you some things about the town, if you're interested. For instance, our friend Carlene Moss runs the local newspaper. She has old typesetting equipment in the printing office that she'd be glad to show you, if she's not busy."

"That sounds like fun," Sidney said. "Can we go, Mom? Dad?"

"I don't see why not," Vaughn said. "Thanks for the idea, Alice."

"You're welcome. Let us know if you need anything."

Louise and Alice walked downstairs and into the kitchen.

"I guess I've never thought much about homeschooling," Louise said. "Though of course I knew there were people who do it."

"It sounds nice to me," Alice said. "*Hmm.* I wonder where Jane is. I assumed she'd be here."

Louise opened the refrigerator and took out a pitcher of lemonade and brought it to the table. She then took two glasses from the cabinet. "I've always thought that children should be in schools with others their own age, progressing year after year until graduation. But I'd say the Campanella girls are keeping up with the world just fine."

Alice accepted the glass of lemonade that Louise offered her. "I'm glad you approve. I've always considered you a diehard teacher—in a nice way, of course."

Louise took a sip of her lemonade, then made a face. "Jane really should have added a little more sugar. I wonder how the Campanellas can teach their children. Though I love her dearly, I never would have attempted to educate Cynthia myself." Cynthia was Louise's thirty-four-year-old daughter who lived in Boston. She worked for a children's book publisher and traveled to Grace Chapel Inn occasionally to visit her mother and aunts.

"The Campanellas seem particularly close to their children," Alice said. "Most teenagers try to stay as far away from their parents as possible."

"You're right on both counts there," Louise said. She

spooned two teaspoonfuls of sugar into her glass. She took a sip. "Ahh. That's better."

Alice looked bemused.

"We'd better not tell Jane. I don't want to hurt her feelings."

"My puckered lips are sealed," Alice said.

Jane was squatting at the edge of her garden, or rather what *would* be her garden. The ground had been rototilled and partly mulched, but she had yet to plant.

She didn't want to take a risk and plant too early, but, oh, how hard it was to wait. It was difficult for her to describe to anyone else, but planting the garden in spring was one of her greatest joys. Even more so than the harvest, planting gave her hope. Maybe it was simply getting out of the house and digging her fingers into the earth after the house arrest that winter imposed.

A car honked, and she turned to see someone racing toward her. A teenage girl in jeans and a hot-pink T-shirt was coming toward Jane, her long brown hair flowing free behind her. Sylvia Songer followed her at a more sedate pace, waving at Jane. "Annie?"

Annie pulled up to a stop, all smiles. "You didn't recognize me at first, did you?"

"Why, no."

"Hi, Jane." Sylvia drew up to them. "Annie wanted to come over and say hello to you and to meet Alice and Louise."

"They're inside," Jane said, then turned to Annie. "I see you've already found some new clothes."

"Do you like them?" Annie asked, twirling around for Jane.

"That's the popular look," Jane said diplomatically.

"Oh, good! That's exactly what I want."

Sylvia exchanged a glance with Jane. "Annie, let's go inside so that I can introduce you to Alice and Louise. Then I'll show you around town some more."

"Are you still excited about riding in a car?" Jane asked, remembering how much fun she had had on their trip to Acorn Hill.

"Oh, sure. This is the farthest away from home that I have ever been. I guess that sounds like nothing to you. Sylvia says that you lived in San Francisco, is that right?"

"Yes. I grew up here in Acorn Hill, then went out to San Francisco when I was just a bit older than you are now. I lived there until I returned home to open the inn with Alice and Louise."

"You flew on an airplane?"

Jane nodded, suppressing a smile.

"I guess it costs too much to do that." Annie turned to Sylvia, the question lingering in her eyes.

Sylvia smiled. "I'm afraid so."

"Too bad." Annie shrugged. "Oh well. There's still plenty to do. The problem is that I don't know where to begin."

Jane laughed. "Let's go inside and say hello to Alice and Louise. If you'd like a snack, I have some cookies and milk handy."

"I'd rather have a soda, if you have one. I never get any at home."

"Yes, of course. We keep them for our guests."

Jane led Annie and Sylvia through the back door and into the kitchen. Louise and Alice were seated at the table, discussing the cardboard-boat regatta.

"Look who's here," Jane said. "Louise, Alice, this is Annie Stoltzfus. Annie, these are my sisters, Alice Howard and Louise Howard Smith."

Louise and Alice couldn't conceal their surprise.

"Yes, I'm the Amish girl," Annie said, laughing. "I'm sure you were expecting the *kapp* and the plain dress."

Alice laughed. "I guess we were, Annie. It's a pleasure to meet you. Forgive us our confusion."

"We're very glad that you're here," Louise said.

"And I'm so glad to be here. I can't wait to see what's in the English world."

Louise invited them to sit down while Jane got Annie her soda and cookies.

Alice inquired about what Annie had already seen, and the girl was happy to share her reactions to all her new experiences. She was so animated and enthusiastic that she made the women smile.

"Maybe we'd better get going and let these ladies get back to whatever they were doing," Sylvia said. "We could take that drive through town, if you'd like. We also need to register you for school."

The teenager jumped up from her chair and walked quickly to the door. "I decided to go to school so that I can meet other kids my age and find out what they do for fun. It was nice to see you ladies," she said, waving as she went outside.

Sylvia sighed as she moved toward the door. "I'm glad to see Annie so happy, but I'm not sure I have the energy to keep up with a teenager. I'll keep you all posted on how things are going."

"Please do," Louise murmured. "I have a feeling you'll be quite busy."

Sylvia paused. "I already am. She's so active. She wants to do something every minute. I don't think she's going to be happy helping me with my shop or with any handiwork after all. Yet I promised Hannah I'd keep an eye on her."

"Are you sure signing her up for high school is a good idea?" Louise asked. "The kids at Franklin High are well behaved, but perhaps her mother wouldn't want her exposed to a lot of other teenagers and their worldly influence."

"Hannah gave Annie her full blessing to go to school,"

Sylvia said. "I really don't have enough work at the shop to keep Annie busy. I think Hannah believes it would be better for her to be at school than being idle during the day. Or perhaps getting into mischief, as she calls it."

Alice looked surprised. "Does she think Annie might get into trouble?" she asked.

Sylvia sighed. "She told me that since Annie has fallen for a boy named Henry Byler, her daughter is sometimes a stranger to her. School is the least of Hannah's worries right now."

"Well, I think school is a great opportunity for her to meet others of her own age," Jane said.

"Even if they're at odds with the Amish tradition?" Alice asked.

"I think that's what she is on *rumspringa* for, isn't she? She wants to see what the real world is like, what non-Amish kids do and believe."

Sylvia nodded. "Jane does have a point. Good to see you all, but now I'd better go see about Annie," Sylvia said, then went out the back door.

When she had gone, Alice turned to Jane. "Sylvia is worried about Annie, I'm sure. It's a lot of responsibility to look after someone else's child."

"I'm sure both she and Annie will do fine," Jane said.

"I wonder if the Franklin High kids will voice opinions about the Amish way of life," Louise mused.

"The Amish believe what they do for a reason," Alice said quietly. "And since Annie is basically a guest in our town, I hope that no one tries to influence her otherwise."

"You mean about how she'll spend the rest of her life?"

Alice nodded.

"I've worried about that too," Louise said. "While I was raising Cynthia, I tried to impart my values, beliefs and lifestyle to her. If she were Annie's age and living among strangers, I would not appreciate their trying to change her views. If Annie changes on her own, that's another situation."

"I still say she'll love meeting kids her own age," Jane said. "And I think it will be good for her, whatever lifestyle she eventually chooses."

Louise frowned. "Despite her mother's worries, Annie seems like a very nice girl. She just needs some time to find herself, as your generation used to say, Jane."

"I just had a thought," Alice said. "Do you suppose Vaughn and Allison Campanella would be willing to have Annie join their girls in some of their studies?"

"That's a wonderful idea," Louise said.

"She'd also only be around girls," Jane said. "I think one of her goals is to meet some boys, you know."

"It wouldn't hurt to ask," Louise insisted. "But we'd better start with the Campanellas first."

Vaughn and Allison thought it was a wonderful idea. When they learned that an Amish girl was living in Acorn Hill, even temporarily, they and their daughters had a multitude of questions. "Of course we'd be delighted to have her join us," Allison said. "She would help us learn as much as we would help her."

"I'll call Sylvia and Annie right now," Alice said.

Sylvia was delighted with the suggestion. Alice could hear her through the phone excitedly relaying the idea to Annie. Then she heard low mumbling in response, followed by silence.

Sylvia picked up the receiver again. "I'm sorry, Alice. Annie says that she'd be glad to meet with your guests to discuss Amish traditions, but she doesn't want to study with them. She still wants to go to Franklin High. Thanks for the offer though."

Chapter Seven

$\mathcal{T}$he next morning was Saturday. Louise entered the kitchen, where Jane was busy preparing breakfast for the guests. Louise studied the pots, pans and casserole dishes that Jane had used to work her culinary magic.

"Looks like you're doing more than usual. Any special reason?" Louise asked.

Jane studied a cookbook while she simultaneously reached for a bowl, cornmeal and milk. "I'm trying a new recipe. I thought our guests might want something different."

"I think your breakfasts have always been varied as well as delicious."

"Oh, thanks, Louise, but that's no reason not to stretch," she said.

"Agreed," Louise said, helping herself to a cup of freshly brewed coffee.

The phone rang. Louise reached for the kitchen extension. "Grace Chapel Inn. Louise speaking."

"Hi, Louise," Bella said. "Would you have some time to meet with me and Hank at Mayor Tynan's office this morning?"

"I have a piano lesson in half an hour, but I can be there after that. Why?"

"We were wondering if you'd be able to help us with our Web site development for Acorn Hill."

"But I don't know anything about computers. Why would you want my help?"

"We'd like you to write some of the material for the site and perhaps talk with town business owners about what they'd like to include on their Web site. You wouldn't have to do any technical work," Bella said.

"Wouldn't Carlene Moss be more suited for the job?"

"Perhaps, but she's so busy and often has to run around the county on one of her stories. Of course, you have your piano students and the inn to run, but even so, your schedule is more predictable than Carlene's." She paused. "Mayor Tynan has spoken highly of your writing ability."

"Well . . ." Louise felt flattered. "If that's all you need . . ."

"Then you'll do it?"

"I'll be there right after I give my lesson this morning."

"Wonderful. Thank you, Louise. I think it'll be lots of fun. I can already tell that Hank's a great guy to work with."

After she hung up, Louise couldn't help the small sigh that escaped her.

"Trouble?" Jane asked, looking up from her cookbook for a moment.

"I just committed to helping Hank and Bella work on

the Acorn Hill Web site," Louise said. "I'm not quite sure what I've gotten myself into."

Jane popped something into the oven and shut the door. "What do they want you to do?"

"Some writing, they said. Maybe work with the businesses that will put their information on the Web page."

"That's great, Louise. I think that we should all try things that are outside our comfort zone."

Louise studied her youngest sister. "Is that what the breakfast is all about? Trying something new and unusual? You aren't on one of your stretching-your-mind kicks, are you?"

"Me?" Jane grinned. "I'm always interested in stretching my mind. That's what keeps a person young."

Louise narrowed her eyes. "*Hmm*. A new breakfast...All right, Jane Howard, out with it. What's up?"

"I was thinking about Aunt Ethel and how she felt like she was in a rut. It occurred to me that sometimes I feel that way too." She paused. "I think mostly that I just have spring fever."

"I know what you mean," Louise said. "I always feel a bit restless this time of year too. Make your new breakfasts, then. As long you're not thinking about implementing other changes at the inn. Changes that might be more radical than making corn fritters."

"Well, I thought I might get a few quotes on some additions to the old place," Jane said, then, seeing her sister's worried look, quickly added. "I'm just kidding, Louise. Don't be alarmed."

Louise shook her head. "You'll let me know when the first bulldozer is scheduled to arrive, won't you?"

"Will do," Jane said cheerfully.

After Louise finished her piano lesson, she headed toward Lloyd Tynan's office. The sun was so warm that by the time she'd reached the mayor's office, she wished she had chosen to drive her car instead of walk. She was grateful to reach the cool interior of Town Hall.

Hank looked up from where he sat alongside Bella at her receptionist's desk. "It's warm out there, isn't it?" he asked.

"A little too warm," Louise admitted.

Bella angled a portable fan toward Louise and gestured her to a seat on the other side of the desk. "Here. Cool off a little before we get started. Would you like a glass of water?"

"That would be nice."

Bella got a paper cup and filled it with water from the cooler. "Here."

Louise sipped the water. "Thank you. That's just what I needed."

Hank fiddled with the computer keyboard, glancing up only at the screen. "This weather feels good to me. I can't wait for the first Little League practice. There's nothing like the sun in your face and the wind at your back when you're sliding into home plate."

Louise shivered. She could understand how boys might enjoy getting dirty and sweaty while chasing around a small white ball, but she could never understand the attraction of the game for grown men. "Anyway," she said, "here I am. What would you like me to do?"

Hank never took his eyes off the computer screen, even while he typed on the keyboard. "If you could contact the businesses we've listed…maybe find out if they'd like us to design a Web site for them…for a small fee, of course."

"Our main objective is to get the Acorn Hill Web site up and running first," Bella said, "but we thought it would be nice to offer the businesses a chance to promote themselves."

Louise drummed her fingers on the desk. "You're going to have to start at the beginning with me. I'm not sure I completely understand the benefit of having a Web site for these businesses, let alone one for Acorn Hill."

Hank tapped out a few final keys with gusto as if concluding a symphony. He twirled in his office chair to face Louise and smiled. "The mayor thinks that we should have a Web presence for Acorn Hill so that we can advertise some of the more interesting things about our town. It will benefit the inn, for example, don't you think? When you book guests, you'll be able to direct them to our Web site so that they'll know Carlene has working typesetting equipment they might want to see. Or that there are specialty shops like Nellie's, Wild Things, Time for Tea. They could find Zachary's hours of operation, or—"

Louise held up her hand. "I get the picture. Wouldn't it also be nice to give some general information about the town's history? Like the original settlers and why they chose this land?"

"Wonderful idea," Bella said, scribbling on a sheet of paper. "Can you talk with Mayor Tynan to obtain that information?"

"Or with Dee Butorac, one of Franklin High's history teachers?" Hank said. "She knows a lot about the area."

Bella made some more notes, then handed Louise the sheet of paper. "Is this enough to get you started?"

Louise felt her heart sink. She wasn't confident that she could handle such a daunting task, but she had agreed to the job. "It's definitely enough to keep me busy."

Bella smiled. "Don't worry. Anything you can bring us will be great. Rome wasn't built in a day, you know."

"Uh-oh!" Hank said, glancing at his watch. He gathered papers in haphazard order, shuffling them awkwardly. "Wouldja look at the time? I'm going to be late for Little League practice. Today's our first, and I don't want to be late. Rev. Thompson would skin me alive." He smiled apologetically at the women. "Well, maybe not skin me alive literally, since he is a preacher, but you know what I mean."

"By all means, go, Hank," Bella said, a bemused smile lighting her round face. "I'll make a few more notes. I think we've overwhelmed Louise already."

Hank stopped his paper shuffling. "Hey, Louise, are you heading back to the inn right now?"

"I thought about talking to some of the business owners on my way home. Why?"

"I need to get in touch with Jane and remind her about our practice. She agreed to help us." Hank withdrew a ball cap from his soft-sided briefcase. "Never mind. I'll give her a call on my cell phone and have her meet us at the ballpark. See you ladies later." He dashed out the door, never looking back.

"Well," Louise said, bewildered. "He's certainly a young man in a hurry."

Bella smiled. "All the young folks are like that now, Louise. Too many gadgets and obligations and not enough time. I don't think he'll ever get married or even have a serious girlfriend. He has too much going on."

"It's a shame, isn't it?" Louise asked, shaking her head. "Acorn Hill used to move so slowly that time almost seemed to stand still."

Bella rearranged the papers that Hank had tried to shuffle into some semblance of order. "You can't stop progress. Compared to the rest of the world, Acorn Hill still moves slowly."

"Not as slowly as time for the Amish," Louise said, thinking of Annie Stoltzfus, or at least how she must have been in Lancaster. Annie now seemed like any other teenager. She reminded Bella about Annie's *rumspringa* in Acorn Hill.

Bella's expression grew thoughtful. "The Amish will always have a corner on slowness and lack of technology, that's for certain. Anyway," she said, brightening. "Mayor Tynan said that when Hank and I had finished I could leave for the day. It *is* Saturday, after all, and I'd like to do some baking this afternoon."

"And I might as well get started on this project," Louise said. "There's a lot of ground to cover."

"It's not too much, is it, Louise? I know you're a busy woman."

"I'm glad to help," she said.

The Campanellas loved Jane's breakfast. She had prepared sautéed apples, whole-grain waffles and corn fritters with maple syrup. Fresh-squeezed orange juice filled a pitcher, and a new blend of coffee filled a carafe. The girls requested milk, so she set out whole and skim. She also offered yogurt and fresh fruit.

"What a wonderful breakfast," Allison said, dabbing her mouth with a cloth napkin. "Much more fancy than we're accustomed to," she said.

The rest of the Campanellas murmured their agreement. Vaughn patted his stomach in exaggeration. "I don't know how we can possibly work on our boat today. Girls, why don't we take a walk first?"

"We need to get our boat supplies, anyway," Lauren said. She turned to Jane. "We need corrugated cardboard and paper tape."

"And paint," Allison said. "As an artist, I'm looking forward to that part. I want the girls to be creative."

"We also need caulking," Vaughn said. "That's allowed on the seams and edges, but nowhere else."

"Can you use Styrofoam?" Jane asked. "Wouldn't that help it float better?"

"That's why it's not allowed," Vaughn said. "I've got a copy of the rules upstairs. I'll make several copies for you and your sisters to give to anyone else in town who might like to participate."

The Campanellas headed out, presumably to Fred's Hardware to get their needed supplies. Jane got to work loading the dishwasher and tidying the kitchen.

The phone rang, and she dried her hands before lifting the receiver. "Grace Chapel Inn. Jane speaking."

"Jane, where are you?" Hank sounded excited. "We're getting ready to start our first practice."

"Yikes! I forgot. Let me change clothes and I'll be right there."

Jane ran up the stairs and threw on a pair of shorts, a T-shirt and sneakers. She pulled her hair back and tucked the ponytail through the hole at the back of a Philadelphia Phillies ball cap. She went back downstairs and found Alice, who was just returning from her walk with her friend Vera. Jane told Alice where she was going, then headed for the baseball field behind Acorn Hill Elementary.

It was easy to spot Rev. Thompson. He wore a baseball cap with the Boston Red Sox's signature *B*. He still looked dignified in chino shorts and a white polo shirt, even as he swooped to field a ground ball.

Surrounded by a group of kids, Hank wore a pair of cut-off shorts, a gray T-shirt and a black Pittsburgh Pirates cap. Even though he had a clipboard tucked under his arm, he held a metal bat in his hands and tried to show a youngster how to get the full benefit of a swing.

The field swarmed with boys. Jane knew the age range for the team was between ten and eleven, and she recognized some of them from church. Many of them were also probably in Vera Humbert's fifth-grade class.

Hank spotted her and stopped midswing. "Hi, Jane. Glad you could make it."

"Glad to be here. Hi, kids," she said, waving. Most of them ignored her, half concentrating on their baseball skills and half indulging in daydreams in the outfield or chatting with each other.

"Yeah, we need some organization, don't we?" Hank asked. He handed the bat back to a youngster, who took a tremendous power swing that narrowly missed beaning another child on the head.

Hank took the bat out of the child's hands and blew a whistle. "Okay, everybody at home plate!"

Some responded, but a few lingered in the outfield. Hank blew the whistle again. "EVERYBODY AT HOME PLATE!"

This time all the kids obeyed, some trotting dutifully toward home plate, a few others dragging their feet. "Come on, everybody," Hank said. "We're going to have to do better than that. Now let's line up by age according to height."

Rev. Thompson and Jane smiled at each other. The kids obediently tried to line up, asking each other's age and holding their hands at their heads to judge their height. Finally, they looked at Hank with exasperation.

"I was just kidding," Hank said. "That's just something a famous baseball player, Yogi Berra, might say. Anybody heard of him?"

Some shrugged, and no one said anything. Finally, a boy held up his hand. "Wasn't that a cartoon bear?"

Hank held a hand over his heart in mock surprise. "I'm shocked. Nobody's heard of Yogi Berra?"

Rev. Thompson smiled. "That cartoon bear was named

after Yogi Berra, Benjie. Much as it pains me to say this as a Red Sox fan, the real Yogi Berra played many years for the New York Yankees and is considered one of the best catchers in baseball history. He's also known for his rather, er, interesting expressions."

"Like, 'It ain't over till it's over,'" Jane said, trying to be helpful.

The kids laughed. "That's crazy," one boy said.

"Yes, it is," Rev. Thompson said. "But I'm glad Hank brought him up. Yogi Berra *was* a great player, and while none of us may ever play for a major-league team like he did, we can all do our best. But mostly, we want to have fun, right?"

The team cheered.

"Most of you already know us, but for those of you who don't, I'm Rev. Thompson. My helper here is Mr. Young, who is a whiz with computers and a huge baseball fan."

Hank gave the kids a mock salute.

"And this is Ms. Howard. She runs the Grace Chapel Inn with her sisters."

"Girls can't play baseball," one boy said.

"Actually, they can," Jane said cheerfully, "but I'm here more for administrative support. Right, Hank?"

"Right. Ms. Howard will help keep you guys in order during the game, letting you know who's up at bat next, who's on deck, who's in the hole, that kind of thing. So," he clapped his hands together once, "it's going to be a fun, great season. Let's see a show of hands. Who's a pitcher?"

Nearly every child raised his hand.

Rev. Thompson grinned at Hank. "You can't all be pitchers," the pastor said gently. "A baseball team has eight other players on the field who are equally important. Now let's try it again. Who's a pitcher?"

This time only half of the children raised their hands. "That's a little better," Rev. Thompson said. "You kids will be working with Mr. Young on your pitching skills. But first, we're going to do some drills."

"*Aww.*" A collective groan went up from the boys. "Do we hafta?" someone asked. "I thought we were going to play a game."

"Yes, you have to," Hank said. "This is 'wax on, wax off' time, guys." When the kids looked at one another in confusion, Hank continued. "You must have seen *The Karate Kid*. Remember how his teacher had him wax the car to get in shape, mentally and physically, for doing karate?"

The kids nodded.

"It's the same principle," Rev. Thompson said. "Let's do something called running a W. We'll line up at first base and sprint to the foul pole, then jog to second base. From there, we'll sprint to the other foul pole and jog to third base."

"That makes a W," Benjie said.

"Right," Rev. Thompson said. "So let's line up at first base. Remember, guys, even the big leaguers you see on TV have to do drills. They probably do this one."

Despite the boys' wanting to play a game, they lined up at first base, eager to emulate their heroes. Hank handed Jane the clipboard. "It's all yours now," he said, then jogged with the rest of the group toward first.

"You, too, Ms. Howard," Rev. Thompson called. "You're a jogger. This will be a piece of cake."

Jane set down the clipboard at home plate and joined the line that had formed at first base. Rev. Thompson led the pack and was already at second base, leading the line. The kids ran after him, and he turned around to jog backward. "Who can tell me what the W stands for?"

"Win!" someone yelled.

"That's right," Rev. Thompson said. "When we play our games, we're going to try our very best to win. What does the W stand for if we don't win?"

Except for the sound of pummeling sneakers and panting, no one answered.

"The W stands for whining. Which I don't want *anyone* to do if we lose. We're going to play hard, but we're also going to…what?"

"Have fun," a chorus of boys yelled back.

"That's right," Rev. Thompson said, turning around to

run from third to first base to start the pattern over again. "Let me hear that again, everybody together. What are we going to do?"

"Have fun!" the boys yelled in unison. Hank and Jane joined in.

Jane smiled, feeling the familiar satisfaction of stretching her muscles, the grass underfoot and the warmth of the day. It was already a lovely spring.

Chapter Eight

Despite their reluctance to do drills, the boys had a renewed enthusiasm for baseball and the coming season by the time the team practice was over. Rev. Thompson stressed to them the importance of sportsmanship and told them that if they learned nothing else but that, he would consider the season a success.

"Tell your parents that they're welcome any time at our practices," he said as the boys gathered their bats and gloves to leave. "I want them all to be involved too. Baseball is a family sport."

After the last boy was picked up, Jane helped Hank and Rev. Thompson gather the team's equipment—bases, baseballs and extra catcher's masks—which they stored in a canvas duffel bag. "Where do you keep this?" Jane asked.

"In the basement at the church," Rev. Thompson said. "The Little League association gave it to me, and I have to keep it all season. I found a spot for it that's out of the way. It'll be fine."

"I'd better head home and get cleaned up," Jane said. "I want to check on our guests and their cardboard-boat project."

"Their what?" Hank adjusted his glasses.

Jane explained about the regatta that would be held in Riverton. Then she told him about Grace Chapel Inn's homeschooling guests, the Campanellas, and the girls' study of boatbuilding while they prepared for the regatta.

"That's fascinating," Rev. Thompson said.

"The guests or the boat race?"

"Both. I've never met anyone who homeschooled, and as close as Riverton is, I'm surprised that I haven't heard about the regatta. Do you think our Little League team would be interested in participating? It sounds like just the thing a group of boys would be interested in doing."

"It sounds like a lot of fun," Hank said, "but if they're concentrating on building a boat, they might be less willing to concentrate on baseball fundamentals."

"I suppose you're right," Rev. Thompson said. "It would certainly help to build team spirit, though."

Jane raised her hand. "I think I have a solution. The Campanellas mentioned that entrants don't have to build their boats in advance. There is also a contest for boats built on site with materials that are provided. Each team has two hours to build a boat with little more than corrugated cardboard and tape."

Rev. Thompson stroked his chin. "That's a thought. Participation like that wouldn't require much preparation and yet the boys would have something to look forward to. What do you think, Hank?"

"I think it sounds great." He wiped his brow with the back of the sweatband on his wrist. "I also think it sounds like a great way to cool off. I have a feeling it's not going to get cool again until after summer's over."

"Then it's settled. I'll make up a flyer with the details and send the information home with the boys at our next practice. Do you know the entry requirements and such, Jane?"

She promised to get him the Web address for the regatta, then said good-bye to the two men. Despite her regular jogging routine, her legs ached from the running drills. Fortunately, Rev. Thompson had excused her from the throwing drills, or her arm would probably ache too.

Back home, she found the Campanellas at the rear of the inn under an elm tree. Vaughn and Allison sat on wrought-iron chairs while the girls sat on a blanket on the ground. Vaughn read aloud from a book, and the others listened intently. At the sound of Jane's approach, he stopped reading. "Hello."

"I'm sorry. I didn't mean to interrupt," Jane said.

"That's all right," Allison said. "Although we're all fascinated."

"What are you reading?"

"Are you familiar with the movie *Master and Commander*?"

Jane nodded.

"This is one of the books from the series that inspired the movie. We've been reading them off and on for a while. In fact, the series fueled our interest in shipbuilding."

Sidney hugged her knees. "It's exciting to think of people living and working on those ships. It must have taken a lot of faith to sail. If something happened to your ship, then something would happen to *you.*"

"But how is that different from living in a house on land every day?" Lauren asked.

"On land, if something happens to your house, you can go somewhere else," Sidney said.

"But what if there's an earthquake?" Marsha chimed in.

"That's a good point," Allison said. "What are the differences between living on land and at sea?"

Jane smiled and tiptoed away. The girls were absorbed in the discussion, and she didn't want to disturb them further. She would, however, make a pitcher of lemonade and bring it to the family. The elm offered lovely shade but was not a complete refuge from the heat.

When she brought out the pitcher and cold glasses on a tray, Jane found that the Campanellas had stopped reading and were working on geometry. "I hope my earlier interruption didn't break your concentration on the book."

"Not at all," Allison said, accepting a glass of lemonade. She took a sip and sighed with appreciation. "Thank you. That hits the spot. No, we had been reading the book for quite a while and were ready to move on to something else."

"And that something was math. More specifically, geometry," Vaughn said.

The daughters groaned as one.

"Not their favorite subject," Allison said. "I have to admit it's not mine, either, but fortunately Vaughn is a whiz when it comes to math."

"What do you do when the girls need to learn a subject that you aren't comfortable teaching?" Jane asked.

"There are authorities in every subject who tutor, either as their primary source of income or in addition to their regular jobs," Allison said. "The girls have had a former chemist teach them chemistry and native French and Spanish teachers for their languages."

"We like to teach the girls ourselves as much as possible," Vaughn said. "It's a learning experience for us as well. We all toured Europe last summer, for instance."

"And the year before that, we all did mission work in Central America for a month," Lauren said.

"It sounds like a great way to learn," Jane said. "I'll leave this pitcher with you. Do you need anything else?"

"No thanks," Vaughn said. "We walked around the area this morning and saw Fairy Pond and Grace Chapel and the cemetery. We never did make it to town, though, so we haven't bought the supplies for the boat. Maybe we'll do that this afternoon. After"—he gave his daughters a playful warning look—"we finish this geometry lesson."

"*Aww*, Dad."

"Jane, Alice told us that the Amish girl chose not to study with us," Allison said. "But do you think that she's still willing to talk to us one day?"

"As far as I know," Jane said. "When you go into town, stop at Sylvia's Buttons. Annie's living with Sylvia right now. You can probably find her there."

"Thanks. We'll check in on her."

After Louise left Bella and the mayor's office, she planned to visit some businesses. Then she remembered that Nia had left for her library conference that morning, so she stopped in to see how Malinda Mitschke, her assistant, was doing on her first day in charge.

She opened the front door of the library and was greeted by the usual quiet. *So far so good*, she thought.

When she approached the checkout desk, she saw that no one was behind the desk and that several clearly impatient patrons waited in line. Among them was Florence Simpson, who drummed her fingers on a stack of VHS tapes.

"Hello, Louise," she said.

"Where is the checkout person?" Louise asked.

"That's what we'd like to know," said the man behind Florence. "We've been waiting here for some time."

"It's very odd," Florence said. "Nia is usually right on top of things."

"Nia left town today," Louise said.

"Nia's left town!" Florence exclaimed rather loudly.

Gasps went up from the rest of the line.

Louise held up her hands. "Now, now, she left someone in charge. Don't panic. Let me see if Malinda is in her office."

The elderly man standing in line behind Florence shuffled uneasily. "Well somebody better get here quick. My feet are killing me."

"I'll be right back," Louise promised.

She headed toward the south end of the building to Nia's office. The door was closed, but Louise could see light shining from underneath the door. She knocked.

She heard the sound of papers shuffling, then a hesitant voice said, "C-come in."

Louise opened the door. Malinda was sitting behind the desk, dabbing furiously at her eyes with a tissue. "Malinda!" Louise moved to the young woman and put an arm around her. "What's wrong?"

"Oh, L-Louise!" she said, her eyes filling with fresh tears.

"Now, now, it can't be that bad." Louise patted her shoulder. "Tell me what I can do to help."

Malinda grabbed a fresh tissue and blew her nose. She sniffled once more, then wiped her eyes with her knuckles. "There's nothing you can do unless you know how to run a library."

"What do you mean?"

"Nia only left this morning, and already things are falling apart. The volunteer who was supposed to work at the checkout desk called to say she couldn't make it. Of all days."

"Did you get someone to cover for her?"

"That's why I'm in here, but I c-can't find the list." Malinda looked as if she was about to begin sobbing, so Louise took her hands and looked her straight in the eyes. She'd heard that this kept people from crying, and she hoped it worked.

Fortunately, it did. Malinda stopped sniffling. "It's not that bad," Louise said calmly. "Did you try working the desk yourself?"

Malinda nodded. "But I can't do that and answer patrons' questions, not to mention take care of all the library paperwork. Saturday is our busiest day." She sighed. "I don't know how Nia handles it all."

"Nia has had a little more experience than you. We'll find someone else to work the desk. Let's stop to think about where the list might be."

Malinda searched Nia's desk, and Louise examined a bulletin board in the office. Half hidden behind a flyer for children's story time was the list. Louise removed it from the board. "Here it is. I'll try to get hold of someone. Meanwhile, dry your eyes and go back to the checkout desk. There are some patrons who've been standing there for some time and need your help."

Malinda let out a deep breath. "Thank you, Louise. You certainly came along at just the right time. I don't know why I fell to pieces."

"First-day jitters," Louise said soothingly. "I'll let you know when I've found somebody."

Malinda left, and Louise scanned the list. To her surprise she saw Ethel's name. *How long has Aunt Ethel been volunteering at the library?* Louise wondered.

She dialed her aunt's number. When Ethel picked up the phone, Louise put that very question to her.

"I haven't officially started yet," Ethel told her. "I decided to get out of my rut by doing something new. So I put my name on the list yesterday. Nia asked me to come in next week for training."

"She must have forgotten that she was going out of town, or perhaps she meant the following week," Louise said, then explained about the conference that Nia was attending. "It might be good if you still came in, but someone else will have to train you."

"That'd be fine," Ethel said. "I'd be glad to help out while Nia's gone."

Louise had a burst of inspiration. "I'm trying to find someone right now to fill in for an ailing volunteer. If I can find someone who's experienced to come in, can you come too? Then you could start your training right away. I think Malinda may need all the help she can get."

"Sure, I can make it," Ethel said. "I didn't have any other plans."

"Wonderful, Aunt Ethel. I'll call you back as soon as I can reach someone."

Louise dialed a few more numbers on the list. Unable to reach anyone after making several calls, she started to worry. Then she reached Clara Horn.

"I'd be delighted to help out," the elderly woman said. "Daisy and I were sitting here wondering what we were going to do all day."

Daisy was Clara's miniature Vietnamese potbellied pig, which she liked to outfit in baby clothes and push around town in a baby carriage or walk on a leash.

Louise controlled her alarm. "Clara, I'm afraid you can't bring Daisy to the library."

"Oh, I know," Clara said with a sigh. "Nia doesn't allow me to bring her. She says that service dogs are the only animals allowed in the library. Though I don't know why. Daisy is clean, friendly and well behaved. She never fusses like some of the babies who are brought to the library by their moms." She sniffed.

"At any rate," Louise said, "if you could come in as soon as possible, Malinda would appreciate it. She's swamped with work. I'm going to ask Aunt Ethel to come in too."

"Why?" Clara asked. "Are you afraid I won't do a good job?"

"Not at all. In fact, just the opposite. Aunt Ethel signed up to start her library volunteer training next week, and Nia must have forgotten that she was going out of town. I'd like you to train my aunt at everything the volunteers do at the library." Because Clara and Ethel were such good friends, Louise knew that Clara would no doubt be delighted.

"Certainly," Clara said, affirming Louise's assumption. "I'd *love* to help my dear friend. I'll be right there."

Louise breathed a sigh of relief as she hung up the phone. She quickly called Ethel with the news that Clara would be her mentor. Then she walked back into the main room and saw that the crowd was gone from the desk. Malinda sat behind it, entering information into the computer. When she saw Louise, she raised her eyebrows hopefully. "Did you find someone?"

"Yes, Clara Horn will be in shortly. I also asked my aunt Ethel to come in." She explained about Ethel's needing training.

Malinda nodded. "Your aunt will learn the routine in a snap. All the volunteers do."

"Are you feeling better now?" Louise asked. "You *look* better."

"I think so. I'm still a little unsure about everything I'm supposed to do. Nia left me a monthly report to take care of, and it's time to make a list of new books to consider purchasing. Then there's a whole box of new CDs and DVDs that need to be shelved..."

"That's what your volunteers are for," Louise said. "Maybe you should make a list of all the things that must be done. Let them do what they can, like cataloging the new media, while you take care of the reports."

"That's a good idea," Malinda said. "I'll start a list right now, while I'm waiting for Clara and Ethel."

Louise said good-bye and left the library, consulting her list of businesses to contact about the Web site. She'd have to wait to talk about the library's inclusion until Nia returned.

Confident that the Acorn Hill library would function reasonably well until that time, Louise headed for the newspaper office. Carlene Moss had published the *Acorn Nutshell* for many years, having inherited the business from her father. He originally typeset the paper by hand—hot type, they called it then. Now Carlene laid out the newspaper on her desktop computer with a publishing program and sent the information to a printer in Potterston. The *Nutshell* came out on Wednesdays, and everyone in town looked forward to reading the weekly news. Carlene was a wonderful writer and the paper's only photographer.

Louise reached the small brown-brick building and

opened the frosted-glass door with its gilt-edged block let-
ters spelling out *Acorn Nutshell* in old-style type. When she
entered, she saw Carlene sitting behind her desk. It took a
moment for the editor to look up, but when she did, she gestured toward a chair near her desk. "Sit down a minute,
Louise. I'm typing up the last paragraph of this article."

Louise obediently sat, studying a bowl of fish on the
desk.

"Done," Carlene said triumphantly. "What's new,
Louise?"

"Well, actually, I'm here to talk about something new."

Carlene leaned back in her chair. "Well, you have my
attention. What are you talking about?"

Louise explained about her work with Hank Young and
Bella Paoli. "Not that the *Nutshell* needs more of a presence,"
Louise said, "but we thought you might want a Web site of
your own, for, oh, whatever reason."

"I can give you one. Advertising. That's a *big* reason. I
have to admit that I've thought of creating a Web site for the
Nutshell, but I didn't see the point if no one would look at it.
People will come to it, though, if it's linked to the town Web
site. And I can sell advertising to other local businesses on
my site. It's a great idea."

"Then you're interested?"

"Does Clara Horn's pig look cute in a baby bonnet?"

"That's a matter of opinion, I suppose," Louise said.

"Well, I think she does, and I think the Web site is wonderful. Can Hank create something for me?"

"Yes," Louise said. "Here is a rate card. If your domain is with the town site, he'll give you a steep discount. He says it's easier to do everything at once."

Louise handed her the card with Hank's prices for designing, creating and maintaining a Web site. Carlene nodded. "This looks more than fair. Put me down as interested."

"You're the first person I've contacted," Louise admitted. "And now, you're the first person who's said yes."

"I hope I'm first in line, then, to get my Web site up and running. Meanwhile, I'll start sketching out some ideas."

"I know nothing about creating Web sites," Louise said. "I wouldn't have the first idea about what information to include. Jane worked with a designer on the Grace Chapel Inn site."

"I'll look at the sites of some city papers to see what they include. I know that one element will be the history of the *Nutshell*. Louise, this is going to be such fun. I'm glad you stopped by today."

"I'm glad you're glad," Louise said, laughing. "Now I suppose I'd better take advantage of my free time and try to talk to some other people."

She left the *Nutshell* office and headed up Acorn Avenue toward Time for Tea. When she opened the door, a bell tinkled, and she was greeted by elegant displays of tea sets and canisters of specially blended teas.

Nattily dressed as always, today in a pale-yellow silk shirt and oatmeal linen slacks, Wilhelm Wood, the owner, emerged from the back room. "Hello, Louise. Can you tell me the name of the piece?"

Wilhelm always had classical music playing in his shop, and he and Louise sometimes played Name That Tune when she entered. Louise listened for a moment to the sound of soothing strings and piano. She smiled with recognition. "Sonata for Violin and Piano in E Minor. Mozart."

"You're right, of course, as always," Wilhelm acknowledged with pretend exasperation.

"I love Mozart's music."

"He's one of my favorite composers as well, but now that I know you're a Mozart aficionada, I'll switch to something else when I see you coming. What can I help you with today, Louise?"

"I'm here on behalf of Mayor Tynan." Louise went on to explain the idea to create a town Web site with links to local businesses.

"Sounds interesting," Wilhelm said. "Count me in."

Louise made a notation on her list beside Time for Tea. At this rate, the entire town would be signed up within the next two hours.

Chapter Nine

*L*ouise didn't have time to speak to every business owner in town, but those she contacted were enthusiastic. Some had no idea what they wanted on their Web site. Others had been thinking about a Web site and had a notion of the information they wanted to include.

That night at dinner, Louise told Alice and Jane about her visits to the various businesses and the promising responses that she received.

"It will certainly help the inn if Acorn Hill has a presence on the Web," Jane said as she arranged herbed parmesan chicken, fresh asparagus, and mushrooms in sour cream on three dinner plates. "I don't mind answering our guests' questions about what there is to do in town, but a Web site will help people plan their activities before they arrive."

"Speaking of activities, the Campanellas are certainly keeping busy," Alice said while carrying the dishes to the table. "I saw them heading into town to buy the supplies for their cardboard boat."

"They were drawing up plans the last I saw them," Jane

said. "They put their supplies in the garden shed. When they start building, they can put the boat on the back porch."

The sisters sat down at the table and Alice said grace.

"Theirs is quite an undertaking," Louise said, picking up the conversation. "Though I wonder if homeschooling is as good as a traditional education."

"Oh, Louie, don't be such a stick in the mud," Jane said. "If you could only have heard them discussing ships today. Vaughn was reading *Master and Commander* aloud. The girls were so enthralled with it that Allison told me later they're going to read the entire series. She said their interest in ships was really sparked by the series, and they were hoping to do a learning vacation one day aboard a tall ship."

"I don't consider that true learning," Louise said. "How do the parents know that the girls are retaining any of the information?"

"How do any parents know that their children are retaining half of what they learn in school?" Jane asked. "It makes sense that children will retain information better if it's something they're passionate about."

"It's not as though the Campanellas allow their daughters to run barefoot through the grass all day, Louise," Alice said. "I think homeschooling is a wonderful alternative to public school. Allison told me that homeschooling is just like a private school, only the parents are in charge."

"I'm still not convinced, but we'll leave it at that for now." She took a bite of the chicken and closed her eyes in appreciation. "*Mmm*. This is delicious, Jane. New recipe?"

Jane nodded, because she was in midchew.

"It's a little more gourmet than what you usually cook on Saturday night," Alice said. "Any special reason?"

Jane swallowed. "Actually, it's a fairly easy recipe, and I wanted to have a nice meal with my sisters."

"Well, this exceeds nice," Louise said. "Oh, I didn't tell you about the library today and about Aunt Ethel." She explained about the mild chaos. "I feel so sorry for Malinda," Louise said. "She's quite timid. I'm sure she has the knowledge to run the library, but she lacks the confidence."

"It'd be hard to live up to Nia's standards," Jane said, a touch of sadness in her voice. "When Nia accepted that position, she stepped right in as though she was born for it. She'll be missed."

"Missed?" Alice asked.

Jane was momentarily flustered, but recovered. "I mean, she'll be missed this week. Why did you mention Aunt Ethel, Louise?"

Louise told them about the volunteer not making her shift that morning and Clara Horn agreeing to fill in. "Aunt Ethel's name was on the list of volunteers, but she hadn't been trained yet, so I asked her to come in too. I thought that it'd help to have Clara go ahead and train her so that she could help out during the coming week."

"Aunt Ethel must have taken our advice to find a new hobby to keep her busy," Alice said. "Good for her."

Jane considered this news. "I never thought about Aunt Ethel's working in the library, but I suppose it's a good idea."

"Do I detect a note of skepticism?" Alice asked.

"Well . . . I'm proud of Auntie for trying something new, but the library is supposed to be a quiet place. I always think of Aunt Ethel as a bit . . ."

"Loquacious?" Louise offered.

"Flamboyant?" Alice suggested.

"Well, let's just say that she doesn't seem a natural for that setting," Jane said. "Don't get me wrong, I love her enthusiasm. But when she's passionate about something, she can go a bit over the top."

"I'm sure Clara will help her fit in," Alice said.

Jane stared at her older sister. "You're talking about a woman who dresses up a pig like a baby."

Alice laughed, obviously picturing Daisy riding in the baby carriage. "Clara's an old softie, and so's Aunt Ethel. They'll help the community by shelving those books, and they'll also help themselves in the process."

"We'll see," Jane said.

As was her habit, Louise left first for church, because she played the organ at Grace Chapel every Sunday. She had been the church organist when she was a young woman still living at home and was delighted to regain the position when she moved back to Acorn Hill. It gave her great joy to help the congregation lift their praise to God.

While Louise played the preservice music, Alice and Jane took seats together in a pew. Sylvia Songer entered and sat by herself several rows ahead of the sisters, apparently not noticing them.

"Let's move so that we can sit with her," Jane whispered.

Alice nodded, and they moved to the end of Sylvia's pew. When she saw them, she smiled and slid over to make room. Rev. Thompson entered to stand in front of the altar, and Louise began playing the opening hymn.

Jane wondered where Annie had chosen to worship that morning. There was no Amish community in the area that Jane knew of. Perhaps she had gone back to Lancaster already. Jane scolded herself for not checking in on Sylvia and Annie during the weekend to see how things were going.

Rev. Thompson preached about loving one's neighbor into the kingdom. Jane was awed that he always made the gospel message so fresh, inspiring and relevant week after week. She was so enthralled with his message that she almost forgot her concern for Sylvia.

When the service was over and everyone had left the chapel to gather outside, Jane and Alice drew Sylvia away from the crowd. "Is something wrong?" Jane asked.

Sylvia looked near to tears. "Annie wouldn't come with me today."

"Did her mother want her to attend church with you?" Alice asked.

Sylvia shook her head. "She never said anything about it one way or another. But I don't think she would be happy to know that her daughter is still in bed at my house. It's no wonder. She was out until midnight last night."

"Doing what?" Jane asked.

Sylvia sighed. "I'll start at the beginning. We went to Franklin High on Friday to register her for classes. Some girls her age were in the school office. They all got to talking and I guess they took a liking to her. They asked her to hang out with them Friday after school. They went to the Potterston mall and then to a movie."

"I'm sure she was thrilled," Jane said.

Sylvia nodded. "I know the girls. Well, I know their mothers. They've done business in my shop a lot. So I didn't worry about that too much. And she was home on time, by midnight. I set that as her curfew on weekends."

"That seems reasonable," Alice murmured.

"I thought so. Anyway, she came home right on time and mumbled on her way to bed that she had had a wonderful time and would be hanging out with some friends on Saturday."

"I'm glad she made some friends," Jane said. "That will be good when she starts school Monday, won't it?"

"I don't know. She slept in till almost noon yesterday, then she took off again with the girls for Potterston. When she left, she had a faceful of makeup that she'd apparently purchased at the mall the night before."

"Teenage girls like makeup," Jane said.

Sylvia shook her head. "This was *way* too much. She wore foundation over that beautiful skin of hers, and heavy eyeliner and shadow. I bit my tongue and didn't say anything. She came home late in the afternoon just long enough to change into some new clothes she'd bought and to say they were going out again that night." Sylvia paused. "With some boys the girls knew."

"That's normal for that age," Jane said soothingly.

"I know, and it's not as though she was by herself with the boys. The other girls went too. But if you could have seen the way she dressed…" Sylvia drew a deep breath. "She had on a black T-shirt and a loose, filmy, hippie-looking shirt and ragged, faded-looking jeans and a pair of ugly black . . . *clodhoppers* is the only word I can think of. She looked like a homeless person."

"That's how the kids dress now, Sylvia," Jane said. "The

bohemian look is popular. We used to wear faded jeans and T-shirts too, remember?"

Sylvia shook her head. "This girl is different, Jane. She comes from a different culture with different clothes." Sylvia's eyes welled with tears. "I just feel so bad, because she's my responsibility!"

"I doubt that a change in fashion is going to change her heart," Alice said, laying a sympathetic hand on Sylvia's arm. "I'm sure she's still the same sweet girl."

"I don't know," Sylvia said. "I hate to see her be like every other teen. I didn't even get a chance to talk to her last night. She came in, said a quick good night, then went straight to her room. I tried to wake her up to go to church with me— or any church of her choice—but when I knocked on her door, she didn't answer."

Jane and Alice were silent, digesting Sylvia's news. "I don't know that there's much you can do," Alice finally said. "If she worries you too much, perhaps you should tell her mother and take her back home."

"Hannah entrusted her daughter to me. I can't admit that I've failed!"

"You haven't failed," Jane said. "I'm sure other Amish kids have gone through this too."

"And the majority of them return to their community, ready to be baptized into their faith," Alice said.

"But what if she doesn't?" Sylvia asked, looking from Alice to Jane.

"You only promised to look after Annie, not walk her into the Amish faith," Jane said. "Even her mother can't do that. You're providing a safe place for her to live, a good environment. If she decides she doesn't want to be Amish after all, it won't be because of you."

"But maybe I'm not being strict enough with her."

"You're doing a fine job, Sylvia. If Annie chooses not to become Amish, it will be in spite of your excellent care and nurturing," Alice said. "I'm sure all parents have their doubts about their child-raising abilities at one time or another."

"But I'm starting with a teenager, not a baby. I haven't had any practical training whatsoever. I'm not only unsure about what to enforce but also how to enforce any rules. If I'm too harsh on her…what's to prevent her from running away?"

"But if you're too lenient, she'll think she can get away with things," Alice said. "I see your dilemma."

Jane shook her head. "Don't read too much into this. She hasn't broken the curfew or misbehaved, has she?"

"Well, no."

"If you feel as if you don't know what you're doing or have any questions, you should ask Louise for advice," Alice said. "She's the only one of us who has raised a child."

Sylvia looked relieved. "That's a good idea. And maybe

I should talk to Vera. She raised two daughters. It feels good to have a plan of action again. Honestly, I don't know how parents bring up kids without an instruction manual."

$\sim$

Louise joined them outside Grace Chapel, and Jane invited Sylvia and Annie to dinner. Sylvia tried to beg off, but when she heard Jane was serving beef tenderloin with port-balsamic sauce, she promised to go home and see if she could get Annie dressed and ready to eat.

"Shall we see if Aunt Ethel is available to join us?" Alice suggested.

"Yes, and Lloyd. We can't have one without the other," Jane said.

"That's an excellent idea. I'm eager to hear how her time at the library went yesterday," Louise said.

"And you can give Lloyd the good news about all the Acorn Hill businesses that want to participate in the Web site," Jane said. "I'm actually glad to have extra company. The tenderloin was on sale. I was going to cut it into steaks and freeze what we didn't use, but now we'll have plenty for everyone."

But before Jane began to cook the meal, Sylvia phoned, sounding sad when she announced that she and Annie wouldn't be able to make it after all. Annie was still in bed and Sylvia felt that she shouldn't wake her. "She probably never gets the chance to sleep in at home with all those other children and chores to be done," Sylvia said. "Thank you for the invitation, but we'll have to make it another time."

The sisters were unable to locate Lloyd and Ethel, so Jane cooked three tenderloin steaks. She served them with oven-roasted new potatoes, and green beans with red pepper.

"The meal looks lovely, Jane," Louise said.

Alice smiled fondly at her younger sister. "Yes, you've gone to a lot of trouble just for Louise and me."

"I enjoy it too," Jane said, placing her napkin in her lap. "Although Pastor Ken called another baseball practice for this afternoon, so I'll be rushed for time."

"Alice and I can take care of cleaning up the dishes and table," Louise said.

"How's the baseball practice going?" Alice asked.

Jane told them about the drills they'd all performed. "I hope they get to bat today. Those boys are itching to hit one out of the park."

Louise shook her head. "I suppose it's more fun to play than to watch. I have to admit that I never understood the attraction."

"I enjoy the crack of the bat as much as the next specta-tor," Alice said. "Mind if I wander over after Louise and I clean up? It might feel good to sit on the bleachers in the sun for a while."

"Sure. You'll probably be the only one there, though. No

spectators came to practice yesterday, and since today is Sunday, I'm sure everyone will be only too happy to drop off their kids for the afternoon."

⌒

Jane was surprised when she showed up at the field. Not only were a good number of parents present, but also quite a few others as well.

Hank was tossing a ball back and forth with Lucas Mallow, one of the boys who'd indicated he could pitch. Jane walked over to Hank. "What gives with the crowd?" she asked, gesturing toward the bleachers.

Hank shrugged. "I'm not sure. The parents stuck around, rather than just dropping off their kids as I expected. Then Fred and Vera Humbert showed up. Then Carlene Moss."

Rev. Thompson approached them, dressed in gray cotton workout pants and a white T-shirt. The familiar Red Sox hat was perched on his head. "Hi, Jane," he said. "What do you think of our audience?"

"I think we should sell tickets," she said, laughing.

"Yoo-hoo, Jane!"

Jane recognized the sound of Ethel's voice, and she turned. "Hi, Auntie." She waved, then turned to Hank and Rev. Thompson. "I'd better speak to her before we get started."

"I'll go ahead and give you the clipboard with today's

drills and assignments," Rev. Thompson said. "We're going to break into groups today, with Hank drilling the pitchers. I'll lead everyone else in working on ground balls and pop flies. Of course, we'll all do warm-up drills together."

Jane groaned. "Running the W?"

"You got it." Rev. Thompson smiled.

Jane made her way over to Ethel. Next to her sat Lloyd Tynan, who was grinning from ear to ear.

"What a beautiful day for baseball," he said. "It just makes you feel good to be alive, doesn't it?"

"It's a little warm for my taste," Ethel said, pressing a handkerchief to her brow. "I'm not usually a fan of sports. All that running and jumping and sweating. Not to mention the possibility of injury. Still, it's for the boys."

"What's for the boys, Auntie?" Jane asked, confused.

"Why, our moral support."

Lloyd smiled at Ethel patiently, as one might at a favored child. "Your aunt is a good sport. She doesn't care for baseball, but she's here because I convinced her that we should get out and support this year's Little League team."

Jane gestured toward the rest of the crowd. "You didn't invite all these other people, did you?"

Lloyd laughed. "Not at all. But apparently the warm weather jump-started the springtime yearning that fans experience every year."

Hank cupped his hands around his mouth and yelled, "Jane! We're ready to start."

"Oops. That's my cue." Jane smiled at Ethel and Lloyd. "Don't get too hot out here in the sun, okay?"

"Not to worry," Lloyd said. "Ethel has her boater, and I brought my trusty Phillies cap." He gestured at the one on Jane's head. "Looks like we're rooting for the same team."

"I hope we'll be able to get caps for *this* team," Jane said. "I think one of the things Pastor Ken wants to talk about today is team sponsorship. Has anybody volunteered to support the team?"

Lloyd grinned. "That's another reason I'm here. After practice, I'll need to talk to you and Hank and Pastor Ken."

"Okay. Well, enjoy the show." Jane jogged toward the field.

"Jane!"

At the sound of her name, she turned around. Carlene Moss stood in foul territory, waving at her. "I need to talk to you after the practice about printing the programs. Pastor Ken told me that you're the person I should talk to."

Jane merely nodded. "Will do, Carlene. Are you staying for the whole practice?"

"Wouldn't miss it," she said cheerfully.

Jane headed out—once again—to the team, wondering if *anyone* would miss the practice. It seemed as though the whole town was at the field.

Chapter Ten

*J*ane didn't think anyone would pay attention, but several parents stood up and applauded while the team ran the drills. A couple of the dads called out their boys' names in encouragement.

"Way to go, Jeremy."

"Run, son, run!"

"That's my boy."

When the drills concluded, Jane assumed that the parents would settle down. Pastor Ken split the team into two groups, with Hank taking the pitchers for special practice. The parents in the stands divided as well, according to the assignment of their sons.

Jane stood next to Hank and they both studied the dads, who were huddled in chattering groups. "I never would have guessed that there'd be such parental involvement at this age level," Jane said. "Not that I'm around kids much."

"I'm sure they'll calm down after a while." He scanned the crowds. "Or maybe at least after a practice or two. I've heard it's always this way when the season first starts."

"But the team hasn't even played its first game yet," Jane said.

Hank grinned. "We may have to add crowd control to your list of duties."

Jane laughed. "Nope, not in my job description."

After practice, Pastor Ken dismissed the boys, who headed toward their parents.

"Hold on a minute," Lloyd said, his voice booming across the field. "Before you all head home, Pastor Ken and I have an announcement."

Everyone turned toward Lloyd. When he saw that he had their attention, Lloyd walked over to stand next to Rev. Thompson. "Go ahead, Pastor. You tell."

Rev. Thompson smiled at the group. "As you know, it's customary for one Acorn Hill business to sponsor our Little League team. In exchange for their monetary support, the business name goes on the back of the jerseys. This year, however, everyone must be gripped with baseball fever."

People murmured to one another.

Rev. Thompson held up a hand to regain their attention. "We had so many businesses volunteer to sponsor this team that Hank and I knew it would be difficult to pick one for the honor."

"So you are going to put *all* the business names on the jerseys?" someone hollered good-naturedly.

Everyone including Rev. Thompson laughed. "No, Hank thought of something better. We're going to have a raffle, with every entrant purchasing a ticket. The money will go toward uniforms, shoes, equipment—everything the team needs."

"What will the winner get?" Jane asked.

"He...or she...will get to name the team," Rev. Thompson said.

"So anyone from me on down to a first-grader could name the team," Lloyd said. "I think it will do a lot to create town support, don't you all?"

"It's a great way to make it truly a town team," Vera Humbert said. "Everyone can pitch in."

"Exactly," Lloyd said. "Ethel Buckley has a fish bowl and a wad of tickets here to start us off. Each ticket costs five dollars, and you write your name on it before it goes into the fish bowl. She'll keep the money and the names until next Saturday, at which time we'll draw the winning name. Ante up for your ticket purchase today and all this week. You can buy as many chances as you want."

Parents began pulling out wallets and checkbooks. Hank, Rev. Thompson and Jane moved away from the crowd, as did the players.

"That was a great idea," Jane said. "Look at the enthusiasm it's generating."

"Not to mention the money," Hank said. He turned to Rev. Thompson. "I told you we'd make a lot of dough."

"Yes, and this way we won't hurt the feelings of all the kind folks who offered to sponsor the team."

Jane clapped Hank on the back. "You have the wisdom of Solomon, my friend."

Hank blushed at the praise.

⁀

Alice joined Jane after the practice. "That was fun," she said. "I sat with Vera and Fred. They were both so excited. Many of those boys are in Vera's class at school, and Fred just loves baseball so much."

"I hope he wasn't disappointed that his hardware store wouldn't be the sponsor," Jane said. "I know he's helped out past teams."

"I think everyone was pleased with the compromise. Isn't it wonderful that there were too many sponsors rather than not enough?"

Jane nodded. One of two boys throwing a ball back and forth between them failed to make a catch, and the ball rolled to Jane's feet. She stooped to pick it up, then winced as she rose. "My muscles are killing me. I'm going home to have a warm soak in the tub." She tossed the ball back to the boy.

"Since I'm out and about, I'm going to stop by Sylvia's and see how she and Annie are doing," Alice said. "I wish they'd been able to join us for your wonderful meal today."

"Me too," Jane said. "I wouldn't worry, though. Annie's

just feeling her oats, being away from home, I imagine. I felt the same way when I left Acorn Hill."

"Yes, but you were a bit older and hadn't led quite the sheltered life that Annie has. Still"—she nudged her sister playfully—"I suppose you turned out all right."

"*Oww*," Jane said in mock pain. She smiled at Alice. "Thanks for the compliment."

Alice walked up Hill Street and turned on Acorn Avenue. She had a hunch that she might find Sylvia in her shop, and she was right. She opened the door and saw Sylvia seated at a low table, surrounded by mounds of fabric. A tape measure hung around her neck, and she had a mouth full of pins.

"*Mmmf*," she said when she saw Alice, then gestured for her to come inside.

"I didn't mean to interrupt," Alice said. "I thought you might be here, but I didn't imagine you'd be working."

Sylvia removed the pins from her mouth. "I'm not working for the shop. I'm sewing a quilt for myself. That, of course, I don't consider work. Have a seat...if you can find one."

Alice removed a stack of fabric from a stool and, after drawing the stool closer to Sylvia, sat down. "Where's Annie?"

"She's back at the house...I hope." Sylvia bent over her work, making rapid, tiny stitches as she joined two squares of fabric.

"How are you two doing?" Alice asked.

Sylvia set the quilt aside. "I feel bad about not being able to dine with you ladies at the inn. I'm sorry that Annie wasn't up and about. I could have come by myself, but ..."

Alice touched Sylvia's hand. "It's all right. We can get together any time."

"I know, but I was looking forward to it. I hoped it would help Annie—that seeing all of you together would make an impression."

Alice smiled. "I'm not sure why. We're just a trio of old ladies as far as she's concerned. I do think Jane is right. Annie wants to be around kids her age. My guess is that once she's had her taste of freedom, she'll make the choice to return home."

"I hope so," Sylvia said, pursing her lips.

Alice smiled. "Sometimes I think adults don't give young people enough credit. They often have a lot more goodness in their hearts than we recognize."

"Oh, Alice. You believe the best about everybody. I've been so amazed by the change that's come over Annie in the few days since she's been with me."

"Maybe you should have a talk with her," Alice said. "Sometimes it helps to share your expectations. It also helps teens to see that we adults are human too."

Sylvia gave a little laugh in agreement.

"By the way, I just came from the Little League baseball practice. Have you heard about the team-naming contest?"

Sylvia shook her head.

Alice explained the raffle.

"I suppose I should enter, though I know nothing about baseball," Sylvia said. "If I win, though, that poor team is not taking the name of Sylvia's Buttons. It'd be a terrible name for a boys' baseball team, wouldn't it?"

"It really would," Alice acknowledged with a laugh. "Well, I'd better get going. You take care."

"Thanks for stopping by. I opened up the shop so that I could have some time alone to cool off. Sewing always helps me relax, you know. I feel even better because of your visit." Sylvia picked up the quilt squares. "Is it all right if Annie and I take a rain check on that lunch? You know how I hate to miss an invitation for one of Jane's meals."

"That would be fine," Alice said. "I feel the same way myself. You know, maybe I'll visit Annie before I head home."

"Oh, Alice, that's a wonderful idea. Please go right on over to my house," Sylvia said.

Alice did just that. She rapped on the door, and Annie answered. Her hair was up in curlers, and she was painting her fingernails. Rock music blared in the background. "Hello, Miss Howard," she said, opening the door to let Alice inside. "Miss Songer isn't here."

"I saw her at the store. I actually came by to see you and find out how you're doing."

Annie went over to the CD player and turned it off. Alice was thankful for the sudden quiet.

"I'm doing fine, Miss Howard. Did Miss Songer tell you I already have some friends?"

"She did," Alice said. "Do they seem very different from your friends in Lancaster County?"

Annie waved her fingers on the air to hasten the drying process of the nail polish. "They sure do. They don't have half the chores I had at home. Some of them even have jobs outside the home and get paid for them." She shook her head. "Some of them don't seem to respect their parents very much, though. They talk back to them and sometimes don't do what they ask. That's sad."

"That's difficult for the parents, too, I'm sure," Alice said and Annie agreed.

They continued to chat for nearly a half hour. Annie told Alice more about her new friends and her weekend activities, and Alice told her more about Acorn Hill, about the Little League and even about her work at the hospital.

"Well, I'd better go," Alice said. "I can see that your nails are dry, and I bet you have plans for this afternoon. I just wanted to stop by and say hello. Come see us at Grace Chapel Inn any time."

"Thank you. I will." Annie cocked her head, smiling at Alice. "You remind me of my grandmother. She's been dead for several years, but she was easy to talk to, just like you are."

"That's a lovely compliment, thank you," Alice said. "I hope that you'll feel free to talk to me about anything that's on your mind."

Annie smiled. "I will."

After Alice left Sylvia's house, she met Clara Horn on the street. The elderly woman was walking her pig on a leash. "How are you and Daisy today?" Alice asked pleasantly.

"We're fine, dear," Clara said. "Do you like Daisy's new bonnet? I didn't want her to get too much sun."

Alice bent down to the pig and studied the bonnet carefully. "I like the yellow daisies around the brim. They're so fitting for her name."

"I'm glad you noticed. Most folks wouldn't, but I should have known you would, dear." She gave Alice's arm a gentle squeeze. "Oh, by the way, I have a question for you."

"What is that?"

"I heard that you have some guests at the inn who are entering the cardboard-boat regatta. I've talked to Ethel and Lloyd, and we're interested in participating."

"You are?" Alice hoped her face didn't reflect her astonishment.

Clara nodded. "We decided it'd be fun."

"And I'm sure that it will be." Alice had to give the older citizens credit. They weren't about to sit back and let life pass them by.

"Do you think we could talk to your guests about what's involved?" Clara asked. "I know we'd be competing against them, but I'm not sure that we old folks know what we're doing."

"I'm sure they'd be willing to give you tips, Clara. It's for a charitable cause, after all. And they're extremely nice. I suspect the real reward is in the building process itself rather than the racing."

"Wonderful!" Clara clapped her hands together like a delighted child, startling Daisy. "I'll get together with your aunt and Lloyd, and we'll stop by to see your guests. When it's convenient for them, of course."

"Of course." Alice nodded.

As Clara and Daisy walked away, Alice remembered that she had toyed with the idea of inviting her ANGELs to compete in the cardboard-boat regatta. The more she heard about the event, the more she became convinced that it'd be fun for her girls to participate. If the Little League team entered, too, Acorn Hill would be well represented in the event.

Hank called Louise Monday morning to see if she could meet at Lloyd's office. He and Bella had put their heads together over the weekend and come up with some ideas for the Acorn Hill Web site. They also wanted to hear about her progress with the town businesses.

"People love the idea," she reported when they had gathered at Bella's desk. "I think you'll have plenty of work to keep you busy," she said to Hank.

"I'm more concerned about getting lots of information to link with the town Web site. Good job, Louise."

"Here are some things that Hank and I feel we should have on the site," Bella said, consulting the top sheet of a pad of paper. "One of the links should be to Town Hall, of course. We think it would help to match a face with the town, so Lloyd has agreed that we can use his photo. He'll write a welcome blurb, and we have a shot of the Visitors Center."

"We'll also have a page that shows exactly where we're located in Pennsylvania," Bella said.

"Which we can get from one of the online map services," Hank added.

"We'll have pages for dining and accommodations… that's where Grace Chapel Inn comes in."

Louise nodded.

"We'll have a page for upcoming events, which could include anything from the local high school football game to church socials to town meetings."

"That will help the citizens as well as visitors," Hank said.

"We can also post town council agendas and minutes"—Bella flipped the page—"and a 'Quality of Life' page with links to health care, housing, library, recreation, Realtors, religious groups, clubs and organizations, shopping—you name it."

Louise felt as though her head were spinning. "I can't quite picture how all this will look," she said faintly.

"Not a problem." Hank took the pad of paper from Bella's hands and flipped through several more pages. "Here's a rough sketch I made, see? This is what the home page will look like—"

"Home page?" Louise asked.

"That's what you call the first screen that people see when they type in your URL."

"You-are-ell?"

Hank smiled. "Sorry, Louise. I forget that not everyone's a geek like me. URL stands for uniform resource locator, which is just a fancy way of saying it's the address for something on the World Wide Web."

"Oh." Louise was still not certain that she understood.

"Anyway, this is what they'll see on the home page. Certain sections will be linked...that is, when the viewer clicks on certain words or phrases, it will take him to another Web page with more information. If he clicks on Food and Lodging, for example, it would bring up a page that lists local restaurants and accommodations. If he then clicks on Grace Chapel Inn, it would bring him to your Web page."

The fog seemed to clear a bit for Louise. "I think I understand."

"It's not too difficult," Bella said. "Of course, Hank has to work the magic to make all this happen, but so far, so good."

"One thing, though," Hank said. "I've been looking at a lot of small-town Web sites, and they all seem to have one thing in common. They all have a slogan or a motto. Does Acorn Hill have anything like that?"

"Not that I know of," Louise said. "But you'd think with our town's history that there would be something."

"The town is as old as the American Revolution, isn't it?" Bella asked. "I'm not a native, but I think someone told me that once."

"Yes, it is. There must be something we can use, some phrase that's been connected to the town."

"We could ask Lloyd, but he's out of his office this morning," Bella said. She scribbled a note on her desk calendar. "I'll ask him when he returns."

Louise handed Hank the list of business owners she'd already contacted about the Web site. "I don't know if you want to contact them now or later, after the town site is up."

Hank studied the list. "I might as well go ahead and get some ideas from them about what they have in mind. Some of them already have planned for this, right?"

"That's what they've said. I'm sure they'll be able to give you more information."

Hank folded the paper twice and put it in the pocket of

his shirt. "I'll get right on it. Ladies, Acorn Hill will soon be online and racing down the information superhighway with the rest of the world."

As Louise left Lloyd's office, she thought of Ethel and wondered how her library training had gone on Saturday. She also wondered if Malinda Mitschke was feeling more comfortable in her temporary leadership position, so Louise decided to stop at the library. When she pulled on the door, however, she suddenly remembered that the library was normally closed on Monday as well as Sunday. To her surprise, the door opened. *What is going on here?* she thought. She stepped inside.

Malinda was nowhere to be seen. However, Ethel stood confidently behind the checkout desk, stamping the book of a young girl.

"I loved this book when I was about your age," Ethel said, returning the girl's library card. "Is this the first book you've read by this author?"

The girl nodded.

"Well, she's written many more books—a whole series about this particular character and her friends. If you like this one, there are many more you can read."

"Thank you," the girl whispered, then joined her mother at the exit. The girl hugged the book to her chest, eyes shining as she and her mother left.

Louise watched as Ethel expertly finished entering the information into the computer and saving it to the system. One would never know that she had been trained only two days ago.

Ethel turned and caught sight of her niece. "Hi, Louise. Did you come to check out a book?"

Louise smiled. "I only came to check *you* out, Aunt. I wanted to see how you were doing."

"As you can see, I'm doing fine." Ethel gestured at the checkout area. "I can't thank you enough for getting me to the library on Saturday. I feel downright useful. Like I have a renewed purpose in life. Clara showed me how to check out books, and it's been a breeze. This is much more fun than shelving a lot of old musty books."

"I'm glad you're feeling chipper again, but if you're here, who's shelving the books?"

"Clara said she'd do it for a while, then we'll trade places. I suppose that's only fair."

"Why is the library open today? It's normally closed on Monday."

Ethel smiled importantly. "We decided that we would open as a special treat today. It'll give the town an extra library day. Pretty nice, don't you think?"

"I am not sure, Aunt Ethel. Did anyone check with Nia?"

"Oh, pooh. Why would we want to bother her? She's having a lovely time at her conference, I'm sure. The last thing we want to do is spoil things for her. We've got every-thing under control."

Louise felt a tug of suspicion growing. "Who are *we*?"

"Why, Malinda, Clara and I, of course. We're a team."

"If Clara is shelving books, where is Malinda?"

Ethel shrugged. "I think she's back in her office. I assured her that everything would be fine here, so she said she'd take care of some paperwork."

"I will see you in a minute, Aunt Ethel. On my way out." Louise headed back to Nia's office. Adding an extra day to the library's schedule, no matter how noble, seemed some-what ill-advised in her opinion.

"Louise." Malinda saw her coming and rose from her desk. "It's good to see you."

"You look much better than you did on Saturday. You're all smiles now."

Malinda laughed. "I'm afraid I wasn't too cheery on Saturday. You saved the day, though, not only by getting Clara Horn to come in, but by arranging to get your aunt trained too."

"Are they truly helping, Malinda? I'm particularly con-cerned about Ethel. She may not know her way around Nia's system yet."

Malinda waved a hand dismissively. "She's doing great. Took to the library work like a duck to water. She and Clara even came up with the idea to open today. We would have opened yesterday, too, but it didn't seem right to work on the Sabbath."

"So you didn't check with Nia about opening today?"

"Didn't see a reason to," Malinda said cheerfully. "Ethel said that she would thank us for drawing extra attention to the library, and I tend to agree. It can only help the patrons if we give them an extra day to check out material. Why, we're doing our part for literacy, right here in Acorn Hill."

"Perhaps," Louise said, her skepticism intact. "But I'm sure there are very good reasons why the library is closed two days a week."

"I'm sure five days a week is enough work for Nia, but this is all new to me, so I'm having fun."

Malinda looked so happy, so full of renewed confidence, that Louise didn't have the heart to press the matter any further. "As long as everything is all right," she said, trailing off.

"Couldn't be better. Thank you for stopping in. Clara and Ethel have agreed to come in the rest of this week, so I'm sure we'll get along just fine. Those two women are so sweet. You're fortunate to have such a lovely aunt."

"Indeed I am," Louise said. Ethel *was* an old dear, though she had a knack for occasionally saying or doing the wrong thing. Fortunately, this was only the Acorn Hill Library. How much trouble could two elderly ladies and an inexperienced librarian get into?

Chapter Eleven

*L*ater that afternoon, while Louise was at the mayor's office and Alice was at the hospital, Jane was in the kitchen preparing whole-wheat ravioli when she heard a rap at the back door. Dusting flour from her hands, she opened the door.

"Sylvia! Annie! Come in," she said.

"Thank you," Sylvia said, leading the way. She was wearing a blouse striped in raspberry, white and green, and a raspberry cotton skirt. Annie had on a blue T-shirt that said Foxy, black jeans and heavy eye makeup. Her hair looked freshly cut in a shoulder-length style that was feathered in graduated lengths around her face.

Jane didn't know whether to mention it, but decided that a girl who just got her hair cut wants it to be noticed. "I see you've changed your hair, Annie."

"Oh, this?" She touched the back of her head. "I went to a salon with a friend after school. I decided to get it cut a bit."

A bit? The stylist must have taken off at least ten inches. What will her mother think? "They certainly did a good job," Jane said. "Does she get her hair cut there too?"

"Not a she. He," Annie said, leaning forward. She lifted her chin. "His name is Darren."

Jane gestured at the teapot, and Sylvia nodded. After she put the kettle on, Jane got three mugs from the cupboard. "So, is he cool?" she asked Annie casually.

"I guess." The girl shrugged. "There are lots of cool boys *and* girls at Franklin High."

"I'd forgotten this was your first day," Jane said. "How did it go?"

Annie yawned. "They recommended that I only take a couple of classes to start. They put me in the freshman class since I only attended school through eighth grade. It wasn't much fun, and I'm not looking forward to homework, that's for certain. The kids told me that the teachers really pile it on."

"You had homework back home, didn't you?" Jane asked.

Annie nodded. "Sure. We weren't homeschooled, like a lot of people think. All of us went to a schoolhouse and had the same teacher."

The kettle whistled and Jane poured the hot water into the teapot. "Speaking of homeschoolers," Jane said as she brought a tray with the pot, mugs and a plate of molasses cookies to the table, "you heard we had a homeschooling family staying with us, right?"

Annie nodded, biting into a cookie. "I heard. Sylvia wanted me to study with them, but despite the homework,

I'm happy to be at Franklin High. I'm glad to be around kids my own age."

"I'm sure you are, but I bet your brothers and sisters and your mother miss you," Sylvia said.

Annie stopped, cookie in hand halfway to her mouth. She set it down. "I suppose they do. Of course I miss them, too, particularly Mam."

"You do?" Sylvia asked.

Annie nodded. "Sure. Especially when I think of what life would be like if I leave the Amish community. I haven't been baptized yet, so they wouldn't shun me, but I wouldn't exactly be welcomed by everyone whenever I felt like popping in."

Jane felt as though her heart might break for Annie. She had just realized that if the girl decided on a different lifestyle, she essentially would have to forfeit her family in the process. "When I was a little older than you, I couldn't wait to leave Acorn Hill," Jane said softly. "I was so eager to spread my wings."

Annie opened her mouth as though she wanted to say something but before she could, there was a knock at the kitchen door. Vaughn Campanella stuck his head in the doorway, saw the threesome at the table and said, "Oh, I'm sorry. We didn't mean to interrupt."

"That's all right," Sylvia said. "We were just chatting and catching up."

The Campanellas came into the room. Jane introduced them, then said, "And this is my good friend Sylvia Songer, and this is Annie Stoltzfus."

"The Amish girl," Allison said, extending her hand to Sylvia and then to Annie. "It's so nice to meet you both. Annie, we look forward to talking to you about your culture."

"I'd be glad to talk with you," Annie said. "I just started school today at Franklin High, but I'm available in the afternoons."

"Tomorrow perhaps?" Allison asked. "We're going to work on our cardboard boat for a while right now."

Annie looked puzzled. "Cardboard boat?"

Vaughn explained, and Jane added that many folks in Acorn Hill were interested in the contest as well. "Clara Horn is entering with Aunt Ethel and Lloyd," she said as an aside to Sylvia.

"Really?" Sylvia was obviously trying hard not to laugh. "That's an interesting picture. I have to admire their spirit though."

"I agree," Jane said.

"We knew your town was getting interested because several people have already asked us for contest information and boatbuilding tips," Vaughn said. "I think some of them are not looking to build seaworthy vessels so much as humorous floats. They were closemouthed, of course, since we're technically their competition."

"It sounds like a wonderful event," Sylvia said. "Oh dear, look at the time, we'd better be going. It was nice to meet you all. Jane, thank you for the tea."

"So we'll see you tomorrow?" Allison asked Annie.

"I'll be here," she promised, smiling.

Jane thought her cheerful expression was quite a contrast to her sophisticated haircut and heavy makeup, but it was good to know the girl was happy and that she was willing to extend herself to others.

After they left, Jane offered to prepare a snack or something to drink for the Campanellas, but they declined. "We're just getting started on our boat. Would you like to see?"

Jane glanced at the ravioli that she had been preparing. Fortunately, the pasta could keep just a bit longer. She was eager to see what they had built so far. "I'd love to."

"Right this way," Vaughn said, gesturing toward the back door.

Outside, Vaughn and his family led Jane to a stack of cardboard. "We got this from the hardware store and various places around town," Allison said.

"Lots of appliance boxes," Sydney said cheerfully.

"We also have tape and scissors," Allison said, "and once the boat is put together, we'll need paint, of course."

"What kind of design will you use?" Jane asked.

"We can't decide," Lauren said. "We can build something that looks conventional, like a luxury liner—"

"—or a kayak or canoe or paddle boat," Marsha added.

"Or we can go for something that looks decidedly *un*shiplike," Lauren said. "Like a space shuttle or a Hummer."

"It doesn't even have to look like a ship or vehicle at all," Vaughn said. "Some folks have created floating computers, soft-drink cans, musical instruments—you name it. It's all about creativity."

"The only rule is that you be able to float it in the pool from the starting line to the finish line," Allison said. "Unless you're going for the *Titanic* award."

"That's the one you win when you have the most impressive sinking, right?" Jane asked.

"Right," Sydney said. "We took a vote, and we know for certain that we want to be able to win by crossing the finish line."

Jane stared at the stack of cardboard and wondered how the family of five was going to be able to make a boat that would not only float but hold them as well. "Have you at least narrowed down your ideas?"

"We're working on a few things," Lauren said mysteriously.

"Right now we're working on calculating water displacement," Vaughn said. "That is, taking into account our combined weights and the least amount of cardboard that it will take to hold us. We don't want our boat to be too big, after all."

"That would slow us down during the race," Allison said.

"I think all that is just designed to get us to study physics and math," Marsha said, wrinkling her nose.

Everyone laughed.

"Well, once we calculate that, we'll probably build a few small-scale models out of heavy construction paper or light cardboard," Vaughn said. "Just so that we know what we're doing when we start the actual building."

"It all sounds fascinating and complicated at the same time," Jane said. "I'm looking forward to seeing what you—and everyone else—come up with."

"Each entry will be individual, I can guarantee you that," Allison said. "That's what's so much fun about this race."

"Are these races a relatively new thing?"

"No," Vaughn said. "In fact, Allison and I saw one of the earliest races way before the kids were born. They originated at Southern Illinois University. An art-and-design professor challenged his freshman class with a creative final examination—to create a life-size boat made strictly of cardboard. The project caught on, and now it's done all over the country for charitable events, fund-raising, team building, community spirit—you name it."

"Of course you know our reason for participating," Allison said.

Jane nodded. "I think it's a great way to build family unity and"—she winked at the girls—"to learn about math."

"Speaking of which," Vaughn said, shooting a mock stern

look at his daughters, "we'd better put our heads together and figure out what we want to do. It's time to get started on our model."

Jane smiled. "That's my cue. I need to get back to dinner anyway. Keep me informed about how you're coming."

Chapter Twelve

*W*ednesday morning, Louise and Alice decided that they both needed haircuts, and so they headed for Betty Dunkle's hair salon, Clip 'n' Curl. Betty preferred that her customers make appointments, but she'd take walk-ins if she wasn't too busy.

When Alice pushed open the front door of the salon, she was greeted by the familiar smells of perm solution and hair spray. These chemical odors were ameliorated by vanilla-scented candles burning on a side table inside the entrance. Posters of hair models hung on three walls, and country music served as background for the sounds of a hair dryer.

Tapping one foot in time to the music, Betty hovered over Florence Simpson, who sat in one of the two barber chairs set in front of the large mirrors on the fourth wall. Betty turned when she heard Alice and Louise come in and waved her styling comb at them. "Hi, girls," she said, her short blond hair bobbing around her round face. "Are you here for cuts?"

"If you have time," Alice said.

"Sure. I'll be with you shortly. Have a seat." She gestured toward the cracked leather chairs in the waiting area on the other side of a glass-block divider.

The sisters waved to Florence in the mirror, and in reply, she fluttered the black nylon cape that covered her.

Betty chatted with Florence while she combed out and sprayed her hair. "So anyway, I'm buying at *least* ten raffle tickets," Betty said proudly.

"For the Little League team?" Florence asked, looking at Betty in the mirror. "What will you call the team if you win?"

Betty shrugged. "How about the Curls?"

"*The Curls?* What kind of name is that for a baseball team?"

"I don't know, Florence," Betty said pleasantly. "If major-league teams can call themselves the Red Sox or the White Sox, I guess a team can be named after a hairstyle." She laughed.

"Well, I'm certainly not interested in naming rights, but I'm behind the team," Florence said. "I think organized sports are a great way to keep kids off the streets."

"They're only fifth-graders, Florence. They're a little young to be juvenile delinquents."

"You never know. Kids get rowdier earlier nowadays, don't they?"

"Oh, I don't know. Most of them are pretty well

behaved." Betty studied Florence's hairdo, then gave it a final spritz. "All finished. Want to check it with the hand mirror?"

Florence nodded, and Betty turned the chair so that Florence could check the back of her head. She nodded her approval. "It looks fine."

Betty unsnapped the protective cape and removed the towel from around Florence's neck. "There you go."

Florence laid her payment on the counter and patted her hair. "It looks nice," she said. "Thanks, Betty."

"See you next time. Alice? Louise? Let me sweep up here a bit, then I'll take whichever one of you wants to go first."

As Alice and Louise rose from their seats, Florence asked, "Are you two backing the baseball team?"

"Of course," Louise said. "In fact, Jane is helping Pastor Ken and Hank with the practices."

Florence raised an eyebrow. "She's not *coaching*, is she?"

"No, she's more like administrative help," Alice said. "But she's doing all the drills with the boys."

Florence shook her head. "I don't know how that sister of yours stays in such great shape. She's not a spring chicken anymore, after all."

"She's fifty," Louise said. "It's not as though she has one foot in the grave."

"Well, of course not," Florence said, smiling. "Fifty sounds younger all the time."

Florence said good-bye, and Betty disposed of the hair she'd swept up. "Who wants to go first?"

"Go ahead, Alice," Louise said. "I'll sit in the vacant barber chair so we can talk. If that's all right, Betty."

"You bet it is." Betty snapped open a clean cape while Alice sat in front of the shampoo sink. "I'm open to any lively news either of you has to relay. Say, I heard that Pastor Ken and Hank volunteered to coach the Little League team when no one else stepped up, but I didn't know about Jane. How did she get involved?"

Alice told the story while Betty washed her hair. Then she moved to the barber chair next to Louise. The *snick snick* of the scissors punctuated their conversation as they discussed the contest.

"Would you really name the team the Curls if you won?" Louise asked.

"Heavens, no!" Betty said, chuckling. "I just said that to get Florence going. I have no idea what name I'd pick. I just wanted to support the team by contributing toward the raffle tickets. I love baseball. As long as I don't have to work, I'll be at every game."

"I'm sure the boys will appreciate that," Alice said over the noise of the blow-dryer.

"There were quite a few people at the last practice," Louise said. "Were you there, Betty?"

She shook her head, studying Alice in the mirror. "I

couldn't make it. What do you think, Alice? I just gave it a bit of a trim."

Alice turned her head from side to side. "I like it, Betty. Nice job. Louise, it looks like you're up to bat."

As Betty brushed stray hairs off Alice's neck with a big, soft makeup brush, Louise rose. "I don't think I've ever been up to bat. I don't recall ever playing baseball as a kid."

"You're kidding! Not even softball?" Betty asked.

Louise shook her head, settling into the chair by the sink for her shampoo. "I don't think that girls played sports when I was in school other than kicking a ball around during recess."

"But it's America's favorite pastime," Betty said. She draped a cape around Louise's neck, then winked at Alice. "We'll make a fan out of you before the season's over."

When Louise's hair was finished, she and Alice paid Betty and said good-bye. The day was so beautiful that they decided to take the long way home, down Acorn Avenue and around the block. When they passed the library, Louise paused. "Do you mind if we stop in? I'd like to see how Malinda's getting along."

"Sure, that's fine. I hope Nia's enjoying the conference," Alice said as they entered the building.

"I hope the library is—what in the world!" Louise exclaimed.

Standing on a step stool, Clara Horn was methodically removing books from the adult section and handing them down to Ethel, who was placing them on a library cart. In the children's section, many of the books had already been removed and were stacked on the plastic play tables and small beanbag chairs. A few patrons browsed the CD, DVD and video lending section or sat at the cubicles against the east wall. Malinda was nowhere to be seen.

"Aunt Ethel," Alice called. "What are you and Clara doing?"

"Excuse me?" Ethel turned. "Oh, hello, Alice. Louise. What did you say?"

Alice and Louise walked toward the elderly ladies. "What are you doing?" Alice repeated.

"We're reorganizing while Nia is gone," Clara said. "We thought it would be nice to have a section for senior citizens, so we're moving some of the adult books to the children's area."

"The shelves are lower there, which makes it easier for us old folks to reach," Ethel said.

"I am sure that's true," Louise said, "but should you be doing this without Malinda's permission?"

"Oh, she knows," Ethel said. "You want to hand me that large book up there, Clara? Yes, that brown one." Clara handed it down, and Ethel groaned under its weight. "Why in the world do publishers make books so bulky? It's impossible to read when you can barely hold it in your hands. Let's just set it aside. Maybe we can put it in the back room. Why, you could put two books in the amount of space this one takes up."

"That's the complete works of Shakespeare," Louise said. "I am sure that someone needs it occasionally."

"Perhaps we should go check on Malinda," Alice murmured to her sister, then said louder to Ethel and Clara, "Ladies, why don't you take a break for a while? We'll be right back, then we can chat."

"I am a little tired, Ethel," Clara said, stepping down from the stool. "Let's sit down."

When they saw that the elderly women were settled, Louise and Alice headed for Malinda's office. "What are they thinking?" Alice asked. "Do you believe Malinda knows what's going on out here?"

"I know she has a lot of paperwork," Louise said. "I'm inclined to believe that she has no idea what they're up to."

She knocked on the door. "Come in, it's open," Malinda said. When Louise and Alice entered, they saw that she was hunched over her desk with a stack of papers. She glanced up, smiling when she saw them. "Hello."

"Do you know what Clara Horn and Ethel Buckley are doing?" Louise inquired gently.

Malinda's face fell. "What do you mean? Aren't they reshelving books?"

"It depends on what kind of reshelving you mean," Alice said.

Now Malinda looked confused. "I don't understand. They said they wanted to help by reshelving. Is there a problem? They seemed so eager to help."

Despite the chaotic situation, Louise felt the urge to laugh. "They are reshelving, but they're moving some of the adult books into the children's area. It seems that they think the lower shelves would be easier for senior citizens to reach." Louise finally had to give in to a chuckle. "They said that you knew all about it."

Malinda's face turned white. "Oh my goodness! I had no idea. I would certainly never have had them do something like that." She rose and headed for the door.

"If they put the books back, no harm will have been done," Alice said soothingly. "I'm not a trained volunteer, but I'm familiar with the Dewey decimal system. I'd be willing to double check that the books make it back into the right spot."

"I'll help too," Louise said.

"We know you're busy, and we want to help you while Nia's gone," Alice added.

"I don't know that I'm cut out to be a head librarian. I'm having a difficult time understanding this management paperwork, and obviously I'm not doing very well at leading people either."

"I'm sure the rest of the week will be fine," Louise said calmly. "Don't be hard on yourself."

"You're right. It's only a few more days, after all. I'll go talk to Clara and Ethel." Malinda paused. "Are you sure you two want to help undo the mistake they've made?"

"We're glad to help," Alice said.

The three went back into the library. Louise thought that Malinda paused extra long before approaching Ethel and Clara, as though she couldn't believe the damage that had already been done.

Malinda put a smile on her face. "Hello, Clara. Hello, Ethel. I see you've done a lot of work."

"We have," Clara said brightly. "Do you approve?"

Malinda's smile faded. "Unfortunately, while I love your innovative thinking and resourcefulness, we're going to have to put the books back where you found them."

"But *why*?" Ethel asked.

"It makes perfect sense to us," Clara said. "And you did say we could reshelve books."

"Yes, but I assumed you understood that I meant to reshelve the returned books to their proper places. Switching adult books to the children's section would benefit our senior readers, but what about the children? They would be confused when they couldn't find their favorite books in the usual location."

"I didn't think about that," Clara said, her face falling.

"Children can't reach books on the higher shelves either," Malinda continued, "even with the step stool."

"I didn't think about that either," Ethel said. She looked at Clara. "We certainly wouldn't want to cause trouble for the kids."

"I know you wouldn't," Malinda said. "So if you'll put the books back in their proper order—"

Clara laughed. "That could take quite a while."

"Louise and I will help," Alice said.

"You don't have to do that," Ethel said. "I'm sure you have better things to do."

"We don't mind," Louise said. "The job will go faster with four of us working. I'm sure we'll be done in no time."

Three hours later, the books were back in their proper places. While Ethel and Clara sat in two of the library's arm chairs, Alice and Louise scanned the shelves to check the Dewey decimal numbers on each book's spine. Finished at last, Louise rubbed her eyes. Her vision seemed slightly blurred as she sank into a chair at one of the cubicles. Alice collapsed beside her, looking similarly stunned.

"Then Daisy did the cutest thing," Clara said loudly to Ethel. "Do you want to hear about it?"

"Of course I do," Ethel said. "I love to hear about that darling."

Louise looked at Alice. Did the two elderly women even realize the trouble they'd caused? "I'm ready to go home," Louise said. "How about you?"

Alice nodded.

Malinda walked up to the sisters. "It's time for the library to close, ladies." She leaned down closer to whisper, "Thank you for fixing that sticky situation."

"It's time to close?" Alice glanced at her watch. "Oh my goodness, I have an ANGELs meeting tonight at the church. We'd better get moving, Louise."

She rose and gestured to Ethel and Clara. "Ladies, it's time to go home. The library is ready to close."

"Oh dear," Clara said. "And we still have so much to chat about."

"Clara, you can come to my house for dinner," Ethel said. "And of course we'll be here tomorrow."

Malinda frowned. She cast a glance at Alice and Louise as though imploring them to intercede. It was clear she was worried about letting the two elderly women loose in the library again. "Maybe we should let one of the other volunteers help out," she said gently. "You two shouldn't do all the work."

Clara smiled. "I already called them and said that Ethel

and I had it covered for this week. We don't have anything else to keep us busy."

Louise felt torn. She knew that the volunteer work had lifted Ethel's spirits, but could she and her friend be trusted to follow orders tomorrow?

Malinda obviously felt that she didn't have a choice. "All right," she said in a small voice. "I'll see you tomorrow."

Home again at the inn, Alice was glad to see that Jane had dinner on the table. She would have to rush to make the meeting with the ANGELs. Fortunately, she had prepared a craft for them and already worked on her lesson. Tonight they would talk about faith and would paint the word on small rocks that could be placed on their desks at home as a daily reminder.

She would also broach the subject of entering the cardboard-boat regatta. Whenever she could, she encouraged the girls to step out of their comfort zones. It would certainly be out of *her* comfort zone, and she knew that some of her girls would feel the same way. Several of them were intimidated by anything that pertained to sports or involved a competition with boys. She already knew that the Little League team planned to compete in the regatta.

"Your haircuts look nice," Jane commented, passing au gratin potatoes to Alice.

"Thank you," she said, accepting the dish. "Betty was all excited about the Little League team."

"Even Florence Simpson said she was looking forward to the baseball season," Louise said, spooning dilled carrots onto her dinner plate. "I never realized how much this town looked forward to it every year, but it's certainly true."

"I'm convinced that part of the allure of baseball is that it begins during spring," Jane said. "Everybody loves to see spring arrive—green shoots of grass, baby birds, flowers budding..."

"It is a lovely time of the year," Alice said. "And the smells of the game are part of that too—the chalk, the grass, the leather—"

"The hot dogs in the vendor's box," Jane said with wide eyes.

"Not that I'm a fan," Louise said, "but when I watched a game or two, I always liked hearing the umpire yell, 'Steee-rike!'"

"I like to hear the organ playing 'Take Me Out to the Ball Game,'" Jane said.

Alice dabbed her mouth with her napkin and laid it aside. "Thank you, Jane, for the lovely meal. I'd love to stay and chat, but I'm late to my ANGELs meeting. Maybe we can catch up more when I get home?"

"Sure," Jane said. "I'll look forward to it."

Alice met with her girls in the Assembly Room, located in the basement of Grace Chapel, while midweek worship services were held upstairs. Alice had founded the middle-school girls' group years ago. It brought her great joy when a former ANGEL, now a young woman, would tell Alice how much the weekly meetings had meant. The meaning of the acronym ANGEL was a secret only Alice and her girls knew, and so far no former member had divulged the information.

Alice always thought that she got just as much out of the meetings as the girls did, and the weekly themes, crafts and songs often lifted her spirits or gave her insight into occurrences in her own life.

Tonight, while each girl painted a rock with the word *faith*, Alice read Bible verses that contained the word. "What happened to some of the people in these verses who had faith?" she asked, after reading the last verse.

"Some were healed," Ashley Moore said.

"Some were rewarded," Linda Farr said.

"Does your faith have to be large?" Alice asked.

"No," Sissy Matthews said. "It can be as small as a mustard seed."

Alice smiled. "Do you know how small that is?"

The girls looked up from their work, shaking their heads. No one had actually seen one.

"I didn't even know mustard grew from seeds," Kate Waller said. "I thought it just came in plastic bottles."

Everyone laughed.

"A mustard seed is very, very small," Alice said, holding her thumb and forefinger closely together as though holding a seed.

After they'd discussed the subject a little longer and almost finished with their rocks, Alice brought up the subject of the cardboard-boat regatta.

As she expected, most of the girls shook their heads to decline and offered reasons for not participating: building a boat would be too difficult; there'd be too much competition; they might drown.

Alice overcame the last objection with the reassurance that they would be able to stand up in the water, and the rules required the participants to wear life jackets. She paused. "Are you girls afraid to compete?"

They looked at each other guiltily. At last Jenny Snyder shrugged and said, "I guess we are."

"We don't have to do it, of course. The registration money does go to charity, but we can always donate money to the cause, if you'd prefer." Alice said.

Ashley set down her paintbrush. "But it wouldn't be the same thing. Maybe we just need to have faith that we can do this. That is what you taught us, right, Miss Howard?"

"Yes, but the decision about entering the competition is strictly up to you. I think it would be fun, but frankly, it's as foreign to me as it is to you girls. I don't know anything about building a boat, cardboard or otherwise."

Ashley stood up at her place to get the other girls' attention. "I think we should try this. We don't have to build it in advance. We can enter the contest where you build a boat at the regatta. Didn't you say that some people build wacky boats, Miss Howard? Since we're ANGELs, maybe we could build an angel boat . . . with wings."

"And maybe a halo," Kate said.

Alice laughed. "I like your idea of building an angel-shaped boat."

All the girls got into the spirit of the discussion, talking loudly over each other. Alice finally raised her voice to be heard over the din. "Shall I fill out the application papers then?"

The girls broke into a unified cheer, and then continued their plans.

⌒

Back home again, Alice met up with Louise and Jane in the living room. Jane had fixed a pot of herbal tea and was curled up on the sofa reading a culinary magazine. Louise sat in one of the chairs, glasses perched on the end of her nose, studying her monthly music periodical.

Jane looked up as Alice sat in the other chair. "How did it go with your girls?"

Alice slipped out of her shoes. "Just fine. They want to enter the regatta."

"This is going to be fun. Lots of people from Acorn Hill are getting in on the act. Are they going to build their boat in advance or build it on site?" Jane asked.

"On site. Which means we still need to have some idea of how to do that." Alice laughed and looked over at Jane. "Do you know where we can get a crash course in shipbuilding?"

Chapter Thirteen

Thursday after school had let out, Jane met Rev. Thompson, Hank and the team at the ballpark for another practice. Even though it was a weekday afternoon, Jane was amazed that, again, many parents and other interested citizens had shown up.

Rev. Thompson worked with one group of the boys, drilling them on fielding ground balls. Hank was off to the side with three other boys whom Jane recognized as potential pitchers. She wandered that way to observe.

"That's it," Hank said as one boy threw a ball into a pitching net and it hit squarely within the target. "Good job," Hank said. "You must have been practicing at home."

"I have been," the boy said proudly. He nodded toward the stands. "My dad's been working with me."

"That's great," Hank said. He looked up and saw Jane. "Hello there. Ready for another day of drills and thrills?"

"I think I'm finally getting used to running the Ws," Jane said. "It certainly gives my jogging a new dimension."

Hank laughed, then leaned closer to whisper. "I don't

want the boys to hear, but we're forgoing running the Ws today to play a game."

"Really? That will certainly please the boys. It should be fun."

Hank scuffed a toe against the grass. "I, uh, hope you say the same thing when I tell you what Pastor Ken and I want you to do. You, uh, don't have to say yes, of course . . ."

"I thought you wanted me to be the dugout manager. Tell the kids what order they're batting in, who's up, who's on deck . . . stuff like that."

"Oh, we do," Hank said, "when we're in real games. But we need you for something, er, special today."

"Bat boy?" Jane guessed.

Hank shook his head. "Would you consider being the umpire?"

"*What?*" Jane was no expert on baseball, but even she knew the grief umpires got. *Hey, Blue, check those glasses! Hey, Ump, that was a strike! No, that was a ball!*

She shuddered. "Why me?"

Hank gestured toward the stands. "I don't see how we can ask any of the parents. They'll want to watch their kids. We wanted someone connected with the team too. Just for this game."

"Well . . ."

"It's really not that hard," Hank said, his voice taking on

a pleading tone. "It'll be good experience, won't it? Plus, you get to wear the groovy outfit."

"You mean that heavy chest protector and the ugly face mask?"

"Rats, someone told you." Hank grinned. "Whaddya say, Jane?"

"Sure, why not? As long as you promise no one will throw food or anything else at me."

"I can't promise that," Hank said, "but it seems like a decent enough crowd, don't you think?"

Jane knew that people could get really worked up, but it *was* just a pickup game, after all, the first chance for the boys to play together.

Hank jogged over to give Rev. Thompson the good news. The pastor beamed at Jane, then gestured her toward home plate. He rifled through the canvas duffel bag to pull out the protective equipment that she knew would be hers.

"Thanks for doing this, Jane. It will give Hank and me a chance to get a good look at the players and decide which boy is best for which position."

"Oh, it's my pleasure," she said, hefting the large chest protector into place. Rev. Thompson buckled it for her, and she sighed as she put on the mask. He helped her adjust it. "How do I look?" she asked.

"Great," he said, smiling.

Jane groaned.

"What's the matter?" he asked.

"I just remembered an old baseball song."

"'Take Me Out to the Ball Game' or 'Casey at the Bat'?" he guessed.

Jane shook her head. "'Nobody Loves the Ump.'"

Rev. Thompson laughed, then asked, "Wasn't that song on an *I Love Lucy* episode?"

"Yes, the one with Bob Hope. Ricky and Bob were doing an act at Ricky's club, and Lucy—"

Hank cleared his throat. "I hate to interrupt your trip down memory lane, but the kids are getting antsy. They want to get started. Shall we choose teams?"

Rev. Thompson called the boys to home plate, then told them they would choose sides for a game.

The boys looked at one another. They were both excited and a little nervous.

"Mr. Young and I will each coach a team, and Ms. Howard has agreed to be our umpire."

The boys looked at Jane with a mixture of suspicion and admiration.

Jane tried to smile reassuringly through the mask but realized her expression couldn't be seen very well.

"Everybody line up along the base path," Rev. Thompson said.

When the boys complied, he counted off, touching each boy's head as he did so. "One, two, one two, one two . . ."

When he finished, there was one boy left over, a small freckle-faced boy who was participating on the team for the first time.

"Do I get to play?" he asked, looking up hopefully at Rev. Thompson.

"Of course you do, Gill. We'll just have two center fielders. Okay, everybody, here's what we're going to do. Other than our pitchers, we're going to let each of you take a different position each inning. That way you'll get a feel for what you like best to play, and we'll get an idea of what position we think each of you is best suited for."

"But I like to play second base," Jeremy Mathers said. "I *always* play second base."

Rev. Thompson looked down at Jeremy. "What if you were better playing a different position and you didn't even know it?" he asked in a kind voice. "Would you want to continue playing second base?"

"No, I guess not." Jeremy looked glum.

Rev. Thompson smiled. "Guys, I know it's hard to have a new coach."

"*Two* new coaches," Hank chimed in.

"Yes, two new coaches. Some of you have played baseball together for several years with the former coaching staff, and you're used to things running a certain way. But in baseball, as in life, you often have to adjust to different methods and to other people. Mr. Young and I are those people while you're playing this year. I hope you'll find that our methods make this game fun for you, not a chore. All we ask is that you play your best. We don't expect anyone to be pro material."

The boys laughed.

He studied his clipboard. "Okay. All the ones are on my team. All the twos go with Mr. Young. He'll give you your first-inning assignments."

The boys crowded around their respective coaches, and someone hollered, "Who gets to bat first?"

"Ah yes," Rev. Thompson said, reaching into his pocket. "Ump, would you mind tossing the coin for us? Mr. Young, it's your call."

Jane tossed the coin into the air. "Heads," Hank said.

Jane caught the coin and turned it onto her forearm. "Heads it is."

"Yay!" Hank's team pumped their fists in the air, then raced for the bats, each one wanting to go first.

"Wait a minute," Hank said. "I need to give your defensive-position assignments first. Then we'll bat in order. Pitcher, catcher, first, second, third . . ."

Jane took the opportunity to study the crowd while she waited for Hank and Rev. Thompson to make their assignments and talk to their teams. Some of the fans were chatting, but others were actively studying the two coaches on the field, following their every move as they arranged the boys either in the field or in order to bat.

"Hey!" One man stood up, "My kid should be playing center field, not left."

"And Stevie should be playing short, not second," another called.

Jane noticed that Rev. Thompson, who could obviously hear the comments, ignored them and went about his business. Hank, who was getting the same amount of grief while arranging the boys in batting order, did the same thing.

When Rev. Thompson and Hank both nodded at Jane that they were ready, she stood behind home plate. But Rev. Thompson motioned for her to join both teams near the dugout. "What's up?" she asked.

The pastor removed his cap and studied the players. "Guys, most ball games begin with the singing of our national anthem. This one is going to start with prayer."

The boys all removed their caps and held them over their hearts. Hank did likewise. Jane removed her catcher's mask and helmet and bowed her head.

Rev. Thompson cleared his throat. "Father, thank You for our time together in this athletic endeavor. We're thankful for our healthy bodies and the beautiful weather. Help each of us to play his best and especially for us all to remember that this is only a sport. While we are having fun, though, improve our character so that we all become good winners and losers, in this game and in life as well. Amen."

"Amen," the others repeated solemnly. The boys looked at one another, shuffling uncertainly.

Jane slapped her helmet and mask back on and returned to her position. "*Play ball!*" she yelled, feeling a certain amount of satisfaction in that all-American phrase.

After Hank's team had beaten Rev. Thompson's team five to three, the parents in the crowd divided into two camps: one enthusiastic and the other frustrated. The fathers and mothers of the kids on Hank's team sang his praises. He was a wonderful coach, an intelligent coach, a skillful coach— hadn't he utilized the boys to the best of their individual abilities?

On the other hand, Jane heard grumbling about Rev. Thompson's skills. Muted grumbles, for he *was* a pastor after all, but complaints nonetheless.

"That was fun," Hank said, whistling random notes while he shoved equipment into the canvas bag.

Rev. Thompson handed him an extra glove to put away. "You're only saying that because your team won," he said, smiling.

"There was nothing wrong with your team," Hank said. "It was just the adage about any given team being able to beat any other given team on any given afternoon."

"What did you think, Jane?" Rev. Thompson asked. "How did you enjoy umping?"

She shrugged, unnerved by the crowd's comments about the coaches. "It was all right. Amazingly, no one questioned any of my calls." *They were too busy questioning the two of you.*

"This game was just for fun," Rev. Thompson said. "All those parents will get even more serious once the real games begin."

Jane pulled the drawstring to close the duffel bag. "I don't know if I'm going to be able to do this anymore."

Hank and Rev. Thompson looked alarmed. "You won't have to ump anymore," Hank said. "This was just a game for fun. Was it that bad, Jane? You said yourself that no one said anything against you."

"No, but they did against you two."

She couldn't believe she had said that out loud, but somebody had to. The two men were working hard and certainly didn't need any abuse.

Hank and Rev. Thompson looked at one another blankly, then turned to Jane. "What's your point?" Hank asked.

"My point? Didn't you hear the crowd talking? Criticizing your every decision? Honestly, for a minute there I thought they were going to complain about the way the field was mowed."

Rev. Thompson gave her a smile. "Jane, you're kind to be concerned about Hank and me—"

"It's not kindness," she said. "I'm angry at those ungrateful parents."

Hank burst into laughter. "You've never worked with a kids' sports team before, have you?"

"No, why?"

"Because if you had, you would know that you cannot please all of the parents," Rev. Thompson said.

"And there will always be those who try not only to second-guess your every decision but also to improve upon it. Coaches just learn to turn a deaf ear," Hank said.

Jane felt deflated. "But how do you put up with it game after game?"

"You learn to tune it out," Rev. Thompson said. "With any luck, we'll have a winning team. And then the coaches will walk on water as far as the parents are concerned."

Jane remembered how the parents of the winning team had praised Hank. "I think you're on to something there. Besides tuning out the criticism, what do you do to get through the games without any parental interruption?

"That's the big question, isn't it?" Hank said with a grin. "If you could bottle the answer, you could market it to every junior sports team coach in America."

"And I," Rev. Thompson said, "would be first in line to buy it."

While Jane was at baseball practice, Louise got a phone call from Bella Paoli. "I have some free time, and Lloyd suggested that I do some work on the Web site," she said. "Is it all right if I stop by?"

"Certainly," Louise said. "Or I would be glad to come to Lloyd's office, if it's more convenient."

"Thanks, but I'd really like to get out in the sunshine and walk a bit," Bella said. "I'll be right over."

Louise brewed a pot of tea and arranged a few of Jane's almond-raspberry cookies and some lemon squares on a pretty china plate. She knew how much Bella liked sweets. Just as she set everything in the living room, there was a knock at the front door. When Louise answered it, Bella was there with a smile on her face, her cheeks pink from the walk.

"Whew! It's good to be out of the office. Thanks for making time for me, Louise."

"It's my pleasure. Please come in and have a seat."

"Thanks." Bella followed Louise into the living room and sat at one end of the sofa.

Louise poured her some tea and passed her the plate of goodies. Bella selected a cookie, took a dainty bite and savored it.

"Absolutely delicious, and they're so pretty, like little linzer tortes. Did you make these?"

"I don't bake much. These are Jane's."

"I wouldn't bake much either if I had a sister who liked

to cook and was as skilled as yours is." As Bella sipped her tea, a thoughtful expression crossed her face. "Being alone, I cook out of necessity, but I do like to bake."

"How is the Web site development progressing?" Louise asked.

"Very well. Hank is experimenting with different looks. We tried to interest Lloyd in helping with the selection, but he pleaded ignorance of Web site design. So it's up to Hank and me to decide, unless, of course, you'd like to cast a vote."

"Not I," Louise said. "I know even less than Lloyd when it comes to such things. I trust you and Hank. Did Lloyd have any knowledge of a town motto?"

"That's what I wanted to talk to you about. He said that he had never heard of one, nor had anyone else I spoke with, and I talked to just about every longtime resident I could find. Lloyd felt that perhaps we ought to ask the town citizens for suggestions. Then we could narrow the entries to, say, the best five and vote on them."

"That's a good idea. We can tap Acorn Hill's creative pool and then let the town decide. *Hmm*. I wonder if we can get Carlene Moss to run something in the *Nutshell*? It wouldn't take much space in the paper, and we could ask people to submit their suggestions to you. You can keep them until they can be voted on."

"Sounds good. Why don't you give Carlene a call right now?" Bella smiled. "Meanwhile, I'll just have another cookie. My sweet tooth hasn't been treated this well in quite a while."

Louise went to the phone at the reception area underneath the main staircase. Carlene answered on the first ring. She was no doubt sitting at her desk as usual, hard at work on the next issue of the *Nutshell*.

"Sure, I can put an item in the paper," Carlene said. "It won't come out until next Wednesday, of course, but the news will start to spread by word of mouth anyway."

She asked a few more questions for the article, then promised to write it up right after she got off the phone. They said their good-byes, and Louise headed back to the living room, where she filled in Bella on the call.

"That's a good idea to spread it by word of mouth," Bella said. "Hank and I will be in touch with all the businesses that you lined up for us, so we can mention it to them then. We can also put up a sign at Town Hall."

"I'll tell Jane and Alice too. They have a wide circle of friends."

Bella snapped her fingers. "We should tell June Carter. I'll bet she and Hope Collins would be glad to tell folks at the Coffee Shop." Bella stood up and smoothed her slim navy skirt. "Louise, thank you for your help. And now, much as I hate to say it, I'd probably better get back to work."

"I'm glad you stopped by," Louise said.

"I enjoyed the walk, our talk and especially"—she

winked at Louise—"the cookies. Please tell Jane how much I liked her baking."

"I certainly will. I know that she'll be pleased."

Louise escorted Bella to the door, where the woman stopped and said, "Oh, I meant to ask earlier about Annie Stoltzfus. How is she doing?"

"The last time I saw her was Tuesday. She was here talking with our guests, the Campanellas. They were eager to talk with her about what it was like to grow up Amish."

Bella smiled. "I could have answered that for them."

Louise's eyebrow rose. "You're Amish?"

"I was *raised* Amish," she said. "It's not something I've ever talked about to anybody in Acorn Hill. I'm not sure why—I don't care if anyone knows, really. But I've never even mentioned it to Lloyd, and he's been my boss ever since he first became mayor."

"I wasn't living in Acorn Hill then," Louise said.

Bella sighed. "I really don't give it much thought anymore, that is, I didn't until I heard about Annie being in town."

"I don't want to gossip," Louise said, "but you might have some special insight. Sylvia is concerned. Annie's completely adopted the modern teenage lifestyle, with the trendy clothes and lots of makeup. Even though Annie's mother sent her here with her blessing, Sylvia feels responsible for the girl."

"I can see why she feels that way, but I'm sure that Annie's mom understands that Sylvia can't make her act a certain way. The purpose of *rumspringa* is for her to decide for herself whether she wants to be baptized." She paused. "Or not."

Louise studied Bella for any telltale emotion. "Do *you* think she should return to the Amish?"

Bella thought for a long time before answering. "That's something she definitely has to decide for herself. There are so many considerations, Louise. To outsiders, I know the Amish life can look enticing. It's a simpler way of life. Families are close-knit. The community pulls together. On the other hand, there's little progress in lifestyle or thinking."

Louise nodded. "I cannot imagine being excluded from higher learning."

"And playing musical instruments," Bella added. "As a music teacher and musician, that would be difficult for you to even contemplate."

"Yes, indeed." Louise shook her head. "I shudder to think of life without the piano or even that cranky old organ at the chapel."

That evening, Louise recounted her conversation with Bella to Jane and Alice. They agreed that they would help spread the word about developing a town motto. When she told them Bella had been raised Amish, they were surprised.

"That's amazing," Jane said. "But then I guess that I never had a conversation with Bella about her childhood."

"Nor I," Alice said.

"I know Paoli is her married name," Jane said, "but somehow I've just always thought of her as Italian by birth, perhaps because of her first name."

"Bella means *beautiful*, doesn't it?" Alice asked.

Louise nodded. "It does seem a bit unusual for an Amish name."

"Maybe it's a short form for something else—like Arabella," Alice suggested.

Chapter Fourteen

The next morning, the sisters all pitched in to clean up after breakfast. When they checked on the Campanellas, eating in the dining room, they found five contented guests. They pronounced Jane's eggs Benedict a work of art.

"Delicious," Vaughn declared.

"Those herbed broiled tomatoes were the perfect accompaniment," Allison added.

"The hash-brown casserole was yummy too," Lauren said.

As Louise and Jane began to clear the table of used dishes, Louise said, "I don't remember your making those dishes before."

"I'm stretching myself, remember? I figure while I wait to plant my garden, I can improve my menu selections. At least I'm not trying to change Grace Chapel Inn itself."

"Don't even consider changing a thing about this beautiful home," Allison said. "It's so peaceful and quiet here, and so comfortable and welcoming."

"Thanks," Jane said. "That's just the atmosphere we try to create." She turned to the girls. "What's on the agenda for you today? What are you doing in the way of classes?"

"We don't ever have classes," Allison said. "We unschool."

"Unschool?" Louise asked, frowning.

"A lot of homeschoolers follow a set curriculum, just like a regular school," Vaughn said. "Unschoolers don't. We allow our children to take the lead in what they want to study. They're self-directed."

"Mrs. Smith, I haven't had a chance to play your piano yet," Lauren said. "Would this morning be convenient for you?"

"Yes, that's fine," Louise said. "I'll be taking care of some administrative work for the inn. If you need anything, just let me know."

"Thanks," Lauren said, beaming.

"As for the rest of us," Vaughn said, "we're going to work on the boat."

"How's it going?" Jane asked.

"Very well. We finally settled on a design and laid out sheets of cardboard and fitted them together. Then we drew the pattern and cut it out with box cutters."

"Now we need to build the ribs to go inside the boat," Sidney said.

"And seal that, then pile on more sealant and tape and assemble everything into a boat shape," Marsha said.

"Then we get to paint," Sidney said. "I'm looking forward to that. Our boat design is basically just a canoe, but we decided we wanted to make it special with paint."

"What will that look like?" Jane asked.

Sidney winked. "It's a secret."

"Would you like to watch us work?" Marsha said. She giggled. "You could do that without spilling the beans about our boat, couldn't you?"

"Oh, it doesn't matter," Sidney said. "We're just being silly. Come on, Ms. Howard. We've put our stuff for the boat on the back porch, like you said we could."

"I'll go play the piano and join you in a bit," Lauren said.

"Let me know if you need me," Louise reminded Lauren. "I'll be working in the reception area."

Louise went to Grace Chapel Inn's work station under the front staircase. Here the sisters kept the main telephone and all their business necessities, including an answering machine and fax.

Louise pulled out a ledger to total a column of figures. Jane had told her that there was software to do this kind of thing in a snap, but Louise preferred the old-fashioned way, enjoying the feel of paper under her hand and a pen in her fingers. She did, however, employ some technology, using a small calculator to help her with the figures.

As she moved from the second to the third column, she heard the haunting strains of the first movement of Beethoven's *Moonlight* Sonata floating from the open parlor door. Her teacher's instincts automatically kicked in, and she set the pen aside to listen. She had heard the piece played many times by many people, and she thought that Lauren's rendition was superb. Technically, the piece was nearly flawless, and her emotional shading was excellent.

Louise tried to make herself go back to work, but Lauren finished the sonata and segued into the second movement of Beethoven's Sonata *Pathétique*. Again, the piece was a teaching standard, but Lauren had obviously practiced until she had achieved performance-level quality.

Drawn by the music, Louise went to stand at the parlor door. Lauren bent over the grand-piano keyboard, lost in the music. When she finished, Louise said, "You play very well."

Lauren looked up. "Thank you," she said. "I hope I didn't disturb your work."

"Not at all," Louise said, moving into the room. "I can see why you want to study music in college. You have a wonderful gift."

"I've had a passion for music for a long time," Lauren said. "Homeschooling's allowed me to spend more time with the piano than if I'd been in regular school seven hours a day.

My piano teacher, Mrs. Stam, has been working with me for years. She thinks I have promise."

"From what I've heard, I concur with Mrs. Stam. I hope you do well with your music studies in college," Louise said. "What would you like to do after school—perform?"

"That would be great, but I think I'd really like to teach. Mom and Dad have always made learning so fun for us, and so has Mrs. Stam. She's hard on me when I need solid criticism, but she also tells me when I've done well. I'd like to be the same kind of teacher for other kids."

Louise smiled. "I understand. That's how I feel too. I know my students most likely won't perform at Carnegie Hall, but if they obtain a lifelong love of music, then I'll consider my job well done."

Lauren smiled. "Thanks for letting me use your piano. Maybe I'd better go help my family with the boat. I didn't mean to disturb you."

"You weren't disturbing me at all. I'm working on some rather tedious accounting, and I appreciate the musical background." Louise smiled. "I understand if you want to get back to your family, but I'd love to hear you play some more. There's a stack of sheet music in the piano bench if you'd like to try something new."

Lauren beamed. "Thank you. I think I will."

Louise returned to the reception area and to the ledger sheets. She put on her reading glasses and sighed. Her heart wasn't in the paperwork, but in the clear, strong notes she heard emanating from the parlor. The accounting had to be done, but she'd prefer to give her full attention to Lauren's beautiful music. She shook her head, squared her shoulders, picked up her pen and reluctantly but determinedly started back to work.

"There you are."

Louise jumped, surprised by her aunt's sudden appearance.

Ethel stood in the reception area, apparently having come in by the back door and through the kitchen and dining room. A pair of glasses with no lenses perched on her nose, and she had somehow managed to work her red hair into the appearance of a bun. She wore a navy cotton-knit skirt and matching overblouse. Dangling from her arm was a large white zippered canvas bag imprinted with pictures of books and cats.

"You startled me, Aunt Ethel. I didn't hear you come in."

"I wanted to surprise you."

"Well, you did. You look a little, ah, different today."

"Do you like my new style?" Ethel patted her hair, revolving slowly for Louise. "I decided that if I was going to be a librarian, I should at least look the part."

"Oh, are you headed for the library?" Louise asked, trying to keep the alarm from her voice. "Will Clara be there too?"

Ethel nodded. "We have a special surprise today, one that I think people will like. Oh, I've had *so* much fun working this week. It's really given me a lift to have something new and helpful to do."

"I am sure Malinda is amazed at what you and Clara have done," Louise said, choosing her words carefully so that they were at once truthful and tactful.

"I'm sure she is. Why, just yesterday she said that she didn't know what the library would be like without us. She's still in her office a lot. She said she had some kind of library inventory report to make, and apparently it's on a software program that she's not entirely familiar with."

Louise made a mental note to see if Hank Young could swing by the library to give Malinda a quick pointer or two about the software. He had helped Nia select and install it, then made himself available as an unofficial "help line." Louise knew that the more Malinda was slowed down by paperwork, the less time she would have to oversee Ethel and Clara.

"How are raffle sales going for the Little League?" Louise asked, steering the conversation toward a safer topic.

"Wonderful, just wonderful." Ethel held up the tote bag. "I had to get rid of the goldfish bowl, and now I carry this around in case anyone wants to buy a ticket."

"You're not carrying around all the money?" Louise asked, alarmed. "I know this is Acorn Hill and not a crime-prone city, but still, one never knows."

"Oh, pooh." Ethel waved her hand. "Who's going to hold up a sweet-looking librarian type like me? Oh, Louise, I can't wait until we draw the name of the winner tomorrow. I'm sure the team is excited too."

"Aunt Ethel, really, about the bag—"

Ethel glanced at her watch. "*Tsk, tsk.* Look at the time. I have to get to the library. Clara will be unhappy with me if I'm late. I promised to teach her how to change the monthly display."

"But it is not the end of the month yet," Louise said, "and Clara has been working at the library longer than you have. Shouldn't she be training you?"

Ethel smiled. "Some folks pick up things faster than others, let me tell you. Oh, it's such a joy to help others. Have a wonderful day, Louise."

"You, too, Aunt Ethel. Maybe I will stop by the library later to see how things are going. Is there any certain time your, er, surprise will take place?"

"I guess it wouldn't hurt to tell you that it should take place just before noon," Ethel said. "We would certainly love to have you there. Say, who's that playing the piano? One of your students?"

Louise shook her head. "No, it is one of our guests."

"I'm not much for classical music, but it sounds pretty good. I wish that I had learned to play the piano. I'm sure I would have been very good at playing show tunes. They're my favorites."

Louise tried hard not to smile at her aunt's braggadocio. She was a loveable old dear, even though she didn't always consider what she was saying... or sometimes, what she was doing.

While Lauren was engaged with her piano practice, Jane followed the rest of the Campanellas outside. The family retrieved their work-in-progress from the back porch and carried it onto the lawn. Just as Vaughn said, they had already laid sheets of cardboard out and fitted them together, then drawn and cut out the pattern. It already looked like a boat, with wider than normal sides.

"We'll fold those in after we put in the ribs," Sidney said when she saw Jane studying the boat.

Because they had set up their materials near the garden, Jane figured she could do two things at once. "I'm going to do some mulching here while I watch you guys, okay?"

"Sure," Vaughn said. "Allison, hand me that pencil, please. Let's measure and draw the ribs."

Jane got the mulch from the garden shed, put on her gloves, and worked the soil. Occasionally she glanced up to watch the two girls and their parents forming the boat supports from more cardboard. They carefully measured and cut out the pieces that would serve as the ribs, then laid them inside the boat. Once the pieces were in place, the family used sealant and tape to attach them.

While they worked, they laughed and joked with each other, discussing the books they'd been reading or information in general that they'd learned about shipbuilding or living aboard a ship. Jane couldn't remember the last time she'd seen parents and teenagers work so closely together in such harmony.

They were finishing sealing the ribs when Jane saw Annie Stoltzfus walk up from the road. Jane set down her shovel and dusted her gloves against one another before removing them. "Annie," she called, waving.

Annie waved back. "Hi, Ms. Howard."

The Campanellas turned. Marsha and Sidney waved at her, and Vaughn and Allison smiled and straightened from where they had been bent over the boat.

Annie sported rather heavy eye makeup for daytime. She wore a bright blue T-shirt tucked into her jeans. "Hi, everybody," she said, plopping down in the grass. "I'm beat."

"No school today?" Allison asked pleasantly.

Annie shook her head. "I'm finished for the day. I only had two classes. To be honest, while I like seeing my friends, I don't care for school." She glanced at Jane, who joined her on the grass. "I don't mean to slam Franklin High, Ms. Howard.

I'm sure it's a fine school. But it's been years since I've been in a classroom. It's hard to sit still on a beautiful day like today. Maybe there's a reason why we Amish don't attend school after eighth grade. It seems like there are more important things I should be doing."

"You're used to being outdoors more, aren't you?" Jane asked. "Right now you'd probably be helping your mother with the garden, right?"

Annie nodded, looking wistful for a moment. "I miss that." She glanced over her shoulder. "I see you're working in yours."

"Yes. I'm doing some mulching."

"My mam's already done that for this year." Annie grinned. "I bet she uses a different mulch, though. Something a little more, um, natural?"

Jane laughed. "I do seem to remember your family having livestock so, yes, I'm sure she's using something different. I buy mine from our local florist."

Annie nodded at the boat. "How's it coming?" she asked the Campanellas. "It looks pretty good so far."

"Thank you," Vaughn said.

"Do you think it'll float?" Annie asked.

Vaughn laughed. "I certainly hope so. Otherwise, we're all going to get wet."

"Well, that might be fun for the spectators, but maybe not for you," Annie said, laughing. "Would it be all right if I come and watch when you compete?"

"Yes, please come," Marsha said. "We're dressing up in costumes and everything. Oops!" She clapped her hand over her mouth. "That was supposed to be a secret."

"That's all right. I think we can trust Annie and Jane to keep our secret," Vaughn said, winking at them.

"Sure thing," Jane said.

Annie nodded. "What kind of costumes are you wearing?"

Marsha looked around as though to make sure no one else was listening, then leaned forward. "We're dressing as characters from *The Lord of the Rings*," she said. She leaned back, a satisfied look on her face, waiting for Annie and Jane to react.

Annie's expression went blank. "Lord of the—what?"

Marsha's face fell. "*The Lord of the Rings*. Didn't you see the trilogy?"

Annie shook her head. "What's a trilogy?"

"It's a story told in three parts, like three books or three movies," Marsha answered.

"Marsha," Allison said gently, "Annie's probably never been to a movie, have you?"

"Just one so far, but that reminds me that I'd like to see more."

"But you've never heard of *The Lord of the Rings* books either?" Marsha asked.

Annie shook her head. "The only reading we do is pretty

much the newspaper, to keep up with current events, or sometimes devotionals."

"Oh, they're wonderful books. I liked them even better than the movies, which were wonderful. It's about a fantasy land where there are sweet hobbits and good and bad wizards and wicked creatures called orcs and trees that walk and talk called ents," Sidney said, her eyes glowing with the memory of the beloved story. "It's about good versus evil, particularly an evil ring that rules over whoever wears it or has it in his possession."

"They were written by a British author, J. R. R. Tolkien, about fifty years ago. Lots of people think of them as three separate books because they have three different titles, but they really make up one story, called *The Lord of the Rings*," Vaughn explained.

"It was made into three movies, which were released in theaters one a year for three years," Allison said. "We loved the books, so we awaited each movie eagerly."

Annie turned to Jane. "Can I go to a theater to see them?"

Jane shook her head. "They're not playing there anymore."

Annie looked crestfallen until Jane added, "But you can rent them. I'm sure Sylvia could get them for you."

"They're very good adaptations from the books," Allison said. "I think you would enjoy them."

"Maybe I will. So you folks are dressing up like charac-ters from the movies . . . er books?"

Sidney nodded. "We have very nice costumes. We're wearing wigs and everything. Dad and Mom are dressing as Gandalf, a good wizard, and Frodo, a hobbit. I get to be Arwen, an elf princess, Marsha's Eowyn, a king's niece, and Lauren's Galadriel, an elf queen."

Annie glanced around. "Where *is* Lauren?"

"She's playing the piano."

"Oh." Annie got to her knees and peered inside the boat. "Do you really think that thing will hold all five of you?"

Vaughn nodded. "We're just about to fold over the sides. Girls, Allison, shall we try?"

They stationed themselves on both sides of the boat and folded the extra-wide sides over to cover the ribs they'd laid along the boat's length. When they had compacted it to fit the boat's shape, crushing and creasing the cardboard, they tackled it with sealant and tape to make it stick.

"Is there a boat in this *The Lord of the Rings*?" Annie asked.

"We've decided to call this the *Grey Ship*," Allison said. "It was gray ships that carried the elves—and other characters—west, into the Undying Lands."

"The *what*?"

"It's a little hard to explain if you don't know the story," Marsha said.

"Oh," Annie said. "I guess I'll understand better when I

see the movies, right? I wonder if Sylvia can rent them for me to watch tonight?"

"I'm sure she can find them, but each movie is at least three hours long," Sidney said.

Annie's jaw dropped. "More than nine hours to watch all three movies?" She shook her head. "The Amish would never understand wasting so much time on entertainment."

"Nine hours does seem like a lot," Jane said, "but these movies are enlightening. They show good opposing evil and how important it is to do right."

Annie looked bewildered. "But doesn't everyone know that?"

Vaughn smiled. "Not in our world. I'm sure you've heard about all the problems that happen outside the Amish community—wars, drugs, disease . . ."

"Sin," Annie added. "That's certainly present in the Amish community too. I think, though—and no offense to any of you—that the Amish take sin a lot more seriously than the English. That's why we do some of the things we do—to make us walk closer with God so that we can avoid sin."

"It'd be nice if more of us English would do that too," Jane said thoughtfully.

"*Jah*. If only a person could live in both worlds," Annie said softly, touching the inside of the boat. "I wish I had a fantasy boat that could take me between both of them whenever I wanted to travel. Or maybe I'd create a land that combined the good from both worlds and left out all the bad."

"If you did, I have a feeling you'd have quite a few people who'd want to sign on as passengers," Vaughn said.

Annie looked surprised. "Why would any English want to be Amish, even only partly? Our ways must seem pretty funny to you. I've seen how people stare at us when we're walking down the streets. I've heard them make fun of our clothes and how we live."

"They're envious," Jane said. "They're not sure why anyone would give up the trappings of the modern life for one so old-fashioned and, to them, quaint. Though they may not understand it, they recognize it as a simpler life and they recognize you as simple people ... a people of faith."

Annie rocked back on her heels. "*Jah*, we are that," she whispered. Though she was still dressed in her modern clothes and makeup, at that moment, she looked to Jane more Amish than ever.

Chapter Fifteen

*L*ouise finished her paperwork and decided that she would go to see Ethel's surprise at the library. It might be prudent for her to subtly check up on her aunt and Clara Horn. But, who knew? Maybe the two women had actually come up with a clever idea.

As Louise got into her car, which was parked in the inn's lot, there was a sudden cloudburst. She instinctively glanced over at the boatbuilders. There was a frenzy of activity as some dragged the boat under the shelter of the big elm tree, while Jane and Vaughn ran to the garden shed. They quickly emerged, carrying a tarp to cover the boat. Then they, too, sought shelter under the thick foliage.

Everything seemed under control, so Louise drove out of the lot and toward the library. By the time she arrived and parked, the rain had stopped. As she began to go up the library steps, several mothers with small children—all very wet—exited the building with some haste.

This can't be good, Louise thought as she opened the door. She stepped in and froze. *Oh no!* The library was a mess and anything but a quiet refuge.

Malinda, Ethel and Clara huddled in the middle of the room while a squawking parrot flew circles overhead. Daisy, Clara's pig, rooted around the library, snuffling at overturned books. In the children's section, a German shepherd barked at a terrified calico cat that was wedged between two shelves of books.

"What's going on here?" she asked the women in a bewildered tone of voice.

Ethel turned to her, wide-eyed. "Clara and I wanted to have a lively story hour with animals, but somehow we just got lively animals."

"We thought they'd behave, but other than my Daisy, they're not," Clara said like a proud parent blind to her child's faults.

Louise drew a deep, calming breath. "Clara, put Daisy back in her carriage, please. Malinda, whose dog is that?"

"M-mine," she stuttered, her eyes filling with tears.

"Why don't you take him home? From the look of things, I believe that the library must close for the rest of the day. Go ahead and take the dog, and I'll put up a sign."

Ethel looked at Louise remorsefully. Her hair had fallen from her makeshift bun. Her glasses sat askew on her nose. "What should I do?"

The parrot squawked overhead, looking for an escape. "Whose bird is that?" Louise asked.

"I borrowed him from Hope, but I don't know how to

get him down. He doesn't seem to want to fly back into his cage on his own."

"Get Hope on the phone and have her come corral the bird. The poor thing is probably terrified."

Everyone moved into action. Once Malinda convinced her German shepherd to abandon the cat and head for her car, Louise was able to rescue the frightened feline and put it in a cat carrier she found in the DVD section. "There you are," she crooned, closing the door. "We'll have you home in no time."

"Hope's on her way," Ethel said. "She said that the Coffee Shop wasn't too busy and that June said she could handle things until Hope rescued her bird."

"Thank goodness," Louise said as she headed toward the checkout desk to make a telephone call to Fred Humbert at the hardware store. She quickly told him what had happened. "We need whatever you'd suggest to clean the carpet and the tile floor. The animals have tracked in a lot of mud." She sniffed the air, which was decidedly pungent with the smell of wet animal. "Oh, and we could probably also use some air freshener."

"I'm glad to oblige. I'll bring everything over in a jiff," Fred said, not quite able to hold back his laughter.

Soon after Louise finished her call to Fred, Hope arrived and coaxed the parrot back into his cage. Tired from his flight to freedom, the bird immediately settled down. Hope took the cage and left, cooing softly to him all the way.

Louise assessed the damage. Books had been knocked off shelves. Displays were overturned. The furniture in the children's section was upended. Mud tracked the carpet and was splashed on books and even some shelves.

Fred arrived with the requested items, and an electric carpet cleaning machine that he rented to his customers. "I thought you might need this," he said, then took in the mess. "I was right."

Louise pushed up the sleeves of her white cotton sweater. "I hardly know where to begin."

Ethel and Clara stood by the checkout desk, their chins lowered nearly to their chests. Louise tried to muster sympathy, but didn't succeed. "What were you two thinking?" she asked, trying to remain calm.

Clara sniffled. "It was story time today, and we wanted to enhance the experience for the kids by having real animals to go with the stories. So we moved the story time to the lawn out back."

"But then it started raining," Ethel said. "Hard. Everyone ran into the library—"

"And brought in the animals."

"The parrot was in his cage and the cat in the carrier, but one of the children must have let them out. We thought we'd be able to capture them, but we were wrong," Ethel said. "Then the dog got excited and started to bark, and Daisy got loose . . ."

"And it turned into a . . . a . . ." Clara faltered.

"Petting zoo?" Louise suggested. "No, I take that back. A petting zoo is much tamer." Her shoulders sagged. "I know you two meant well, but you see how this got out of hand."

"Yes," Ethel said in a small voice. "We were only trying to help. The kids *did* have fun until the animals started going crazy. We'll help clean up, of course."

"Would you like me to stay?" Fred asked. "I can close the store."

"That won't be necessary," Louise said. "You shouldn't have to jeopardize business on our account. I hate to do it, but I'll call home and see if Alice and Jane can help us. But Aunt Ethel . . . Clara . . . I don't think that you should volunteer at the library again."

"But I love working here," Ethel said. Clara nodded her agreement.

"I know you do, but this is twice now that you've created unnecessary work for the rest of us." Louise sighed. "In any case, this isn't up to me. Why don't we see what Malinda says when she returns."

Fred left, and Louise placed a call to the inn. Alice answered and agreed to help with the cleanup. "Let's not ask

Jane to help," she suggested. "She's been working in the garden most of the day."

"Yes, you're right," Louise said. "I think you and I can manage with Aunt Ethel's and Clara's help."

Alice arrived in just a few minutes. After she recovered from the sight, she went straight to work with Louise, Clara and Ethel. Louise assigned Clara and Ethel the easier tasks of straightening books and sweeping the linoleum floor. Alice cleaned up the larger muddy areas and spot cleaned, and Louise filled Fred's machine with its special detergent and shampooed the carpet.

Malinda returned, and quietly went to work righting the upset displays. At last Louise finished with the rug and shut off the machine. As she wrapped up the cord, she caught Malinda wiping a tear from her cheek. "Why are you crying?" Louise asked.

"I'm sure I'll lose my job over this."

Louise put her arm around Malinda's shoulders. "None of us is your supervisor. We don't have the authority to do that, even if we wanted to."

"Yes, but Nia will find out."

Louise prayed for guidance in this delicate situation. "Malinda, it's true that Nia left you in charge of the library and two chaotic things have happened. I know you're strapped for help, but Clara and Ethel were definitely out of line. Their hearts were in the right place, but they didn't think through their ideas."

Malinda nodded.

"I also know that you were trying to help both the library and those two elderly women. It's difficult to say no to them."

Malinda nodded again. "But I should have. I just don't know how to say no. I'm good at organizing books and I'm learning the administrative paperwork, but I don't know that I'm good at leadership."

"Not everyone's a born leader, but leadership is an ability that a librarian does need." Louise considered this for a moment. "I think you must be upfront with Nia about what happened and tell her that you are willing to take a leadership-training course if she thinks that's a good idea."

"Do you think that would help?" Malinda's face lit with hope.

"I believe so," Louise said. "Meanwhile, perhaps it would be best if Clara and Ethel worked independently of each other at the library. One can work the checkout desk and the other can shelve books. No variations. You can start your leadership training by enforcing that."

"I can do that. There are several other volunteers that I've put off because Clara and Ethel were so eager. I'll call them." She paused. "I really thought that Clara and Ethel had good ideas, but I guess not."

Louise put her hand on Malinda's shoulder. "And I know

you were trying to make them feel useful, which they still can be. With direction. Are you up to it?"

Malinda nodded. "I think so. Even if I have to abandon the paperwork, I'll keep a closer watch on them."

Louise glanced at the library, which had finally returned to normal. "Good," she said.

Louise wanted to talk with Malinda a bit longer at the library, so Alice left for home alone. Exhausted from cleaning, she planned to settle down with a book or maybe take a nap. Or better yet, a hot soak. Her muscles ached.

Back home, however, she saw Jane, the Campanellas and Annie Stoltzfus gathered behind the house. She could have ducked inside to rest and no one would have been the wiser, but it looked like such an interesting group. And they *were* working on the cardboard-boat. Maybe she could get some building pointers for her ANGELs.

"Hi, everybody," she said.

The Campanellas looked up from the boat, to which they were applying sealant and tape. "Hi," they said almost in unison.

Jane sat alongside Annie on a garden bench. Jane patted the spot next to her, inviting Alice to sit down.

"Hi, Miss Howard," Annie said, scooting over to make room.

"Thank you," Alice said, a soft groan escaping as she lowered herself gingerly.

"What's wrong?" Jane asked.

Alice explained about the catastrophe at the library.

Jane's mouth twitched for a moment, then she burst out laughing. "I'm sorry, Alice," she said when she could finally speak. "But that's just too funny."

"Ethel and Clara mean well," Alice said, sighing. "But they've been a two-woman wrecking crew at the library this week."

"Do the Amish have such difficulties with their elderly relatives and friends?" Jane asked Annie, still chuckling.

"Sometimes, if they are a little forgetful. Mostly, though, they are well supervised, since they live in rooms attached to the main family house."

"That's rather like Ethel," Jane said. She pointed in the direction of the carriage house. "She lives over there."

"She knows that she's welcome in our home at any time," Alice said.

"And well she knows it," Jane said, smiling. "She's been known to pop over a time or two."

"How convenient," Annie said, returning the smile.

"Have you learned much about boatbuilding today?" Alice asked, gesturing at the Campanellas' work.

"A little," Annie said, "but I can't see the wisdom of

building such a temporary thing. Especially for a contest. We don't believe in competitions. We believe it leads to pride."

"It certainly can," Alice said. "But the race is for charity, though I must admit that my ANGELs want to do well."

Annie stared at her. "You have angels?"

Alice smiled. "That's the name of a group of middle-school girls that I teach once a week. We have Bible lessons and learn verses and do secret good deeds. We also work on arts and crafts or sing. It's a good time for girls that age to be together while we learn about God."

Annie shook her head. "I still don't understand building a boat out of cardboard. My friend Henry Byler works in his father's woodworking shop, and he would be appalled."

Wendell, the Howard sisters' tabby cat, strolled up. Annie called him over by making soft sounds and gesturing with her fingers. He willingly went to her, and she stroked him gently.

Even though she already knew, Jane asked, "Is Henry your boyfriend, Annie?" She wanted to see how Annie would answer.

The girl smiled slowly. "In a way. I know my mam didn't like me hanging out with him. He did get a little wild in the past few months, but I like him," she said softly. "I even dreamed about us getting mar—" She stopped, embarrassed.

"Getting married?" Jane asked softly.

Annie nodded. She continued to pet Wendell, who purred loudly. "When the Amish get married, it's a wonderful thing. The two people must be baptized and an announcement is published in church. Everyone comes to the wedding, and it's an all-day event. The bride bakes her own cake."

She smiled dreamily. "There's a huge feast. Weddings are usually on a Thursday, so that everyone can prepare all week for the event and then have a couple of days to clean up before the Sabbath. The bride wears a brand-new royal blue dress and a white apron that she wears again when she dies and is buried." She grinned. "Of course, I never dream about the *second* time I'd wear the blue dress, but I often think about the first time."

She blushed. "I can't imagine not getting married among the Amish, even though I live with you English right now."

"It must be difficult to live outside your community," Alice said. "Unlike my sisters, I've never lived beyond Acorn Hill. I can't imagine leaving my hometown or the people I grew up with."

"It is hard," Annie said. She kept smiling, though the effort appeared forced. "But there are so many things to enjoy in the English world. I don't know if I can go back."

"Not even for family?" Alice asked softly.

Annie's eyes filled with tears. "I don't know."

Alice put her hand over Annie's. "I didn't mean to upset

you. I'll be praying for God to give you the right direction and that you'll have peace of mind when He gives it."

"Thanks." Annie swiped at her cheeks, then rose. "I guess I'd better head back to Sylvia's. Especially if I want to ask her to rent *The Lord of the Rings* movies for me."

"Oh, I love those movies," Alice said. "What made you think of them?"

The Campanellas went on working, seemingly unaware of the question.

Jane smiled at Annie but didn't say a word.

Annie's mouth curved into a small smile as she tried to keep the Campanellas' secret without fibbing. She shrugged. "I heard about them and they sounded interesting. I'll let you know how I like them." She waved at the group. "Bye, everybody." She turned to Alice. "You really do remind me of my grandmother, Miss Howard. It's comforting to me."

Sidney and Marsha looked up from where they were creasing cardboard. "Bye, Annie. Come back and see the boat tomorrow."

"We'll still be working on it," Vaughn said, wiping his brow.

Alice and Jane left their guests working outside and headed indoors. Jane said that she had accomplished all she could with the garden that day and wanted to start dinner. Alice was ready to soak her tired muscles.

Jane set a kettle of water on the stove for tea. "That was nice of you to help out at the library," she said. She shook her head. "I still wonder what Aunt Ethel and Clara were thinking. Ethel has lived on a farm. She knows what animals are like."

"They were trying to make things more interesting for the children, and it certainly turned out that way," Alice said. She couldn't help the chuckle that escaped her. "You should have seen the inside of the library."

"Actually, I think I'm lucky that I didn't," Jane said, her eyes twinkling. "The smell of wet animals and the sight of mud all over are not for the faint of heart."

"You're hardly that," Alice said to her adventurous sister.

The kettle whistled. Jane poured water into the teapot and added a tea ball full of herbal tea. After it had steeped, she poured a cup of the tea for Alice. "See if this doesn't soothe you."

Alice took a sip. "*Ahhh*. That tastes good. Thank you, Jane. After I finish my tea, I think I'll head upstairs for a relaxing bath and maybe a few chapters of my mystery novel."

Louise entered the back door, looking tired.

"How about some tea?" Jane asked. "I think you've earned it."

Louise sat down with her sisters. "Thank you, Jane. That

would be wonderful." She turned to Alice. "And thank you for helping out."

"Are Ethel and Clara all right?" Alice asked.

Louise nodded, accepting a steaming cup from Jane. "They're fine. Properly but gently chastised as well. They're only to work at the checkout desk or shelve books—the right way—from now on."

"At least Nia will be back this weekend," Alice said.

Louise sighed. "No, she won't."

"What?" Jane plunked down her cup. "Did she decide to move to Pittsburgh?"

Louise and Alice looked at her. "Why would she do that?" Alice asked.

"Because of her boyf—" Jane stopped. "I'm sorry, but I'm not supposed to say anything. I promised."

"Now you've piqued our curiosity, but I know you can't go back on your word," Louise said. "All I know is that she called Malinda just before I left the library and told her that she was staying away longer. She said she wanted to spend some more time there."

"What did Malinda say? She didn't tell her about the mishaps with Ethel and Clara, did she?" Alice asked.

Louise shook her head. "No, thank goodness. No sense in worrying Nia and forcing her to rush home. She said that things were going all right and that she would manage until Nia returned."

Jane stared into her teacup, looking guilty. "I hope she has a good time during her stay. She deserves some time off. She works so hard."

"She does indeed," Louise said. "I think we've all learned this week how invaluable Nia is. Malinda has her heart in the right place, but she needs more experience before she can be left to manage a library on her own. She freely admits that and wants to improve herself. No, I can't imagine the library permanently without Nia Komonos."

Jane held up the teapot. "Would anyone else like some more?" she asked, wanting to change the subject.

Chapter Sixteen

*T*he next morning, Saturday, was sunny and pleasant with a light breeze stirring the leaves. Jane whistled as she prepared breakfast for the Campanellas and her sisters. She wore a white apron over her athletic shorts and white T-shirt.

"Today's the big raffle to name the Little League team, isn't it?" Alice asked, helping Jane by heaping scrambled eggs onto a platter.

Jane nodded. "The boys are so excited, and so are Pastor Ken and Hank and I. Ethel hasn't told us exactly how much money has been contributed, but she says it's a lot. That will buy us new equipment and uniforms, pay for tournament fees…oh, I'm so happy about how everyone in Acorn Hill has pulled for the boys and their hard work."

"Everyone loves baseball," Alice said, "and if there's one thing people love more than the game, it's watching boys having fun playing baseball."

Jane used tongs to arrange a stack of crisp bacon on a platter. The game today had preempted her desire to make a fancy breakfast. "I'm glad the boys are having fun, because I don't think a lot of the parents are. They're always trying to tell Pastor Ken and Hank—and sometimes me, even—how to coach the team. Honestly, you'd think we were trying to win the World Series."

"They are just concerned about their children," Alice said.

"If you ask me, they're *over*concerned. They need to stand back and let the coaches coach. They're trying to do everything themselves."

Both sisters carried trays laden with the eggs, bacon and light, crusty biscuits through the swinging door into the dining room. They set the food on the buffet just as Vaughn and Allison entered.

"Good morning," Jane and Alice said.

"Good morning to you as well," Vaughn said.

"The food looks delicious," Allison added.

"Thanks," Jane said. "I wonder if I may ask you a parenting question."

"Shoot," Vaughn replied.

"I'm helping the coaches of the town's Little League team. Frankly, some of the parents are way out of hand."

"They're trying to do the coaching for the coaches?" Vaughn asked, spooning scrambled eggs onto his plate.

"How'd you know?"

He smiled. "A lot of people think homeschooling parents

are the helicopter type—you know, hovering. The truth is, Allison and I *are* involved in a lot of aspects of our kids' lives, but all the years we've been schooling, we've tried to teach them independence."

"And to appreciate what others can offer, of course," Allison said. "Lauren's piano teacher, for example. We don't interfere with her lessons for Lauren. Same with other teachers or coaches the girls have had through the years."

"Besides, sending the girls to other teachers is often how we keep our sanity," Vaughn said, winking at Jane. "It gives us time to regroup and have some time to ourselves."

"Someday I will probably pursue some of my own interests," Allison said. "I've always wanted to take voice lessons."

"Line dancing for me," Vaughn said. "One day the girls will be in college or pursuing careers away from home, and then Allison and I will have time to study the things we want."

"I admire that you're so involved with your children," Alice said. "You certainly seem to have a healthy attitude toward raising them."

"Some parents don't," Jane said, making a face. "Like some of the Little League parents. Maybe if they home-schooled, they wouldn't feel the need to coach."

Vaughn laughed. "We always say that anyone can home-school, but homeschooling is not for everyone. I'm sure they feel they're helping their children."

"I think they're just trying to *be* their children," Jane said, shaking her head. "But we'll see how things go today."

Allison and Vaughn took their filled plates to the table, then returned to the buffet for fresh-squeezed juice and coffee. "Don't take too much," Allison teased her husband. "The girls will be down shortly."

"Working on the boat again today?" Jane asked.

Allison nodded. "I think we're almost ready to paint."

"If you want to take a break, come over to the baseball field near the elementary school," Jane said. "The Little League team is having a scrimmage today, and we're going to conclude our raffle to name the team sponsor."

"What an interesting concept," Allison said. "Did you get a lot of entries?"

"I believe so," Jane said. "We charged five dollars an entry, so I'm sure we raised a lot of money for uniforms and equipment."

Alice glanced at her watch. "If you'll excuse us," she said to the Campanellas, "we'll leave you to your breakfast. Jane, we'd better get ready for the scrimmage."

Jane consulted her own watch. "Yipes, you're right! Allison, Vaughn, if you'll just leave your dishes on the table, I'll take care of them when I get back."

She and Alice pushed back through the swinging door into the kitchen. Alice headed upstairs to change clothes while Jane did a hurried cleanup of the cooking utensils and cookware she'd used for breakfast. She whipped off her apron, put on her ball cap and headed out the back door. She'd promised Hank and Rev. Thompson that she'd get to the ballpark early for practice.

To her dismay, not only were most of the kids already on the field, but parents were crowded behind the backstop. A couple of the fathers clung to the chain link, shouting directions through the fence.

"Sam, pay attention!" one man yelled.

"Aim a little higher on your next throw, Chris."

Jane shook her head. She walked toward Rev. Thompson and Hank, who stood quietly talking in the dugout. Hank saw her and handed her the clipboard. "Hey, Jane. Here's today's lineup."

She glanced at the players on the field, then nodded at the overzealous fathers. "Are you sure they're going to like this?"

"They may not," Hank said, "but they'll have to abide by it. Besides, it's only a few dads, not all the adults."

"Hank and I have thought very carefully about which position we want each boy to play," Rev. Thompson said. "I hope their parents will understand. We have the boys' best interests at heart."

"Pastor Ken's worked with the position players, and I've worked with the pitchers." He smiled. "It should be an interesting scrimmage."

"I hope everyone feels the same way when the game is over," Jane said.

Soon Rev. Thompson and Hank were huddled with their respective teams, going over last-minute strategy. Jane advised all the standing parents to find seats on the bleachers so that everyone in the stands could see the game. Many other people were already in the stands, even those without kids. Wearing her Yankees cap, Bella took her seat and waved at Jane. Hank saw her and waved back, his own Pirates cap planted firmly on his head.

"I can't wait until we get our own uniforms," Jane murmured, adjusting her Phillies cap. "We look like a hodge-podge of teams."

Louise and Alice sat beside Bella, and Jane saw all the Campanellas join them. She nearly did a double take, for sliding into the bleacher next to them was Annie Stoltzfus, followed by Sylvia Songer. Sylvia waved at Jane, and she waved back.

Jane was thankful that she wasn't the umpire today. Hank had pressed an old college chum from Potterston into service, and Jane was only too happy to see him don the ump's gear. Clutching her clipboard, Jane took her place in the dugout with the boys from Rev. Thompson's group.

They looked at her hopefully. "Some of us are playing

positions we're not used to. Do you think we can win, Ms. Howard?" one boy asked.

"Of course I do," Jane said. "Your coaches know you've been practicing hard. Go out there and do your best."

"I'm going to smack a home run out of the park," one boy said, pointing to the distance, presumably where the ball would land. "My dad told me to."

"Me too," said another. "My dad says I shouldn't bother trying to hit a single. Why just hit so that you only get one base?"

Jane gripped the clipboard, her heart breaking at the determined earnestness on the boys' faces. "Guys, what did Rev. Thompson say was the first thing to remember about playing baseball?"

The two sluggers chewed on their lips, thinking.

A few feet away, Jeremy whispered, "Have fun?"

"That's right. The main thing is to have a good time. This is America's game, guys. If you do well—if you hit that home run, great. But if you don't, just enjoy it. Do your best. That's all anyone can ask. Okay?"

The boys nodded. "I'm still going to swing for the fences," one boy said, smiling. "But I'll try not to be disappointed if I don't get a home run."

She sighed. Maybe she was making *some* progress.

Jane stayed in the dugout during the entire game, keeping track of each team's lineup. While one boy was batting, she told the next batter to take practice swings "on deck." She then alerted the boy who was "in the hole"—or the next batter to go on deck. The coaches had also asked her to keep track of statistics when she could—whether a boy went down on strikes without a hit, or whether he got on base by making contact with the ball or by being walked.

During the early innings, Jane noticed that most of the boys tended to "swing for the fences," as the one boy had indicated he would do. Few of them had any success at even hitting the ball, never mind scoring a home run. As the game wore on, however, the boys seemed to relax and enjoy themselves more. Their swings became looser and easier. Sometimes Jane saw a look of surprise cross the face of a batter who hadn't really expected to make a hit but suddenly found teammates cheering wildly: "Run for first! Run!"

If the boys grew more relaxed in their play, however, some of the parents grew more tense. Jane could hear the patter of mothers in the stands, sometimes discussing the game, sometimes other matters. Two of the fathers—the ones who made a habit of leaning up against the backstop and blocking the view for others—took every opportunity to coach their kids.

"Choke up on that bat!"

"Widen your stance!"

"Don't swing at the first pitch!"

Jane hoped the boys couldn't hear their fathers, particularly when they criticized their sons' play.

None of them stepped up to coach the team when it was apparent that Gerald Morton wouldn't be able to, but they're certainly willing to coach their own sons. She reminded herself that she'd do better to keep her mind on the game and her own responsibilities.

By the last inning, even Jane was beginning to wilt from the warmth of the day. She could barely keep track of the score, and when Rev. Thompson's team had beaten Hank's team, she was more than delighted that the game was over.

The two teams met on the field to shake hands afterward. Some of the parents watched, shaking their heads. "I'm going to have to work harder with my kid," she heard one dad say. "He let a ball get past him that he should have had a glove on immediately."

Jane waited until the coaches had congratulated their teams on working hard, then, while the boys were racing for the sports drinks that one mother had provided, she turned to Hank and Rev. Thompson. "Good game, fellows."

Both their faces were glistening with sweat. "It was fun," Hank said. "I hope the boys had a good time."

Rev. Thompson agreed, then glanced at Jane. When he saw the seriousness on her face, his own expression sobered. "I heard those parents too," he said. "Maybe it's time to hold a parents' meeting."

Hank nodded. "I hoped we wouldn't have to, but a couple of the fathers are getting more and more vocal. When the kids are loose, they have fun and they actually play better. When the dads are wound up, so are the kids. You have to wonder if major league-players ever go through the same thing."

A slow smile crept across Jane's face. "Hank, you may be on to something."

"Who me? What'd I say?"

She patted him on the back. "Let me do some checking, then I'll get back to you both. Don't say anything to the parents just yet, all right?"

"All right," Rev. Thompson said. He tossed a baseball back and forth from his right hand into his gloved left hand. "If there's one thing I've learned about our friend Jane Howard, Hank, it's that she usually has a creative way to solve a problem. If she says to wait, I'm content to do so."

Hank shrugged. "Okay by me. I wasn't looking forward to talking to the dads anyway." He rubbed his hands together. "And now . . . how about a little sports drink for the coaches and the dugout manager?"

"And then we draw the winning ticket," Jane said.

Rev. Thompson nodded. "I can't wait to find out who we're going to be this year."

Hank laughed. "Don't get your hopes up. I don't think it's going to be the Red Sox."

Louise sat in the stands between Alice and Bella. She had waited patiently throughout the game just to be present for the naming of the team. Several times Bella had to explain the intricacies of the game, and, if Louise was honest with herself, she would admit that baseball had a certain appeal.

She certainly enjoyed watching some of her students play something other than piano. When they sat in her parlor, they generally seemed like young gentlemen, all serious and solemn. By fifth grade, they stayed with piano lessons because they wanted to. Mothers could only force their sons to be musicians for so long.

"Wasn't that a great game?" Alice asked. She smiled at Louise. "I forgot. You're not a big baseball fan."

"It was actually interesting. Quite . . . dramatic."

Bella smiled. "It's not everybody's cup of tea, but you tend to like it more if you're familiar with the rules. Lots of folks consider it a thinking-man's game. And the more you learn about it, the more you agree. It's a team sport, but it's also a one-on-one competition between the pitcher and the batter."

The Campanellas, seated behind the three women, leaned forward. "This has been fun," Vaughn said. "We haven't been to many ball games as a family, and this has given us some ideas for lesson plans."

"History of the game, biographies of famous players . . ." Allison said.

"Physics of baseball . . ." Vaughn added.

"Please," Lauren said, then was joined by her sisters in a chorus: "No math!"

Vaughn and Allison laughed.

Louise laughed too. "My goodness. You really *do* turn everything into a learning experience, don't you?"

"We try." Vaughn smiled.

Louise smiled back. She had to admit these homeschoolers knew how to make the world their classroom.

Sylvia and Annie sat farther down, next to the Campanellas. Sylvia leaned as far to the side as she could. "Didn't Jane look good?" she asked.

"She certainly looks efficient," Louise said. "Although I must confess that I'm not sure what she was actually doing in the . . . the, uh . . . what did you call it, Bella?"

"Dugout," Bella said. "I'm sure she was reminding the boys of the batting order."

"It was nice of you to come, Louise," Alice said. "I'm sure you're ready for them to draw the name of the raffle winner."

Louise craned her neck to scan the crowd. "Where *is* Ethel?" she asked. "She has the raffle tickets Pastor Ken will draw from."

"There she is," Alice said, pointing toward the third-base

line. Ethel and Lloyd were seated together, chatting. Ethel gestured wildly with her hands.

Louise rose and said, "I think I'll go over and say hello to Aunt Ethel and Lloyd."

She cut across the bleachers until she reached the section where the couple sat.

Ethel broke off her conversation with Lloyd midsentence. "Why, hello, Louise. What are you doing here? I didn't think you liked baseball."

"Hello, Lloyd. Aunt Ethel. I have to be honest. I came to the game so that I'd be here for the drawing of the team name."

A look of horror washed over Ethel's face. "Oh dear!"

Louise's heart sank.

Lloyd smiled fondly at Ethel. "Didn't I say this very thing would happen?"

"Oh, Aunt Ethel, is the money gone?" Louise asked.

"Gone?" Ethel waved her hand. "Good heavens, no. Louise Howard Smith, I know you think I'm a doddering old fool sometimes, and especially lately with all that library nonsense."

Lloyd leaned forward. "She told me all about that business, Louise. You have my sympathies and my thanks as town mayor for cleaning up one of our public facilities." He winked at Ethel.

"Oh, you." Ethel laughed.

"Aunt Ethel, what about the money?"

"Oh, *that*. Why, it's at home. Just before we left for the game, I told Lloyd that I should put all the names back in the goldfish bowl so that we would have something presentable to draw from. I didn't want to bring all that money to the game. I realized that you were right. That it could easily be stolen. Or misplaced."

"So...the money is at your house? The bowl is there too?"

Lloyd nodded. "Looks like I need to make a trip to the carriage house. Ethel, if you'll give me your key, I'll go pick up the bowl. I know right where you left it. No need for you to make the trip. You can stay here and chat."

"Thank you, Lloyd," Ethel said.

"Yes, thank you," Louise added.

Car keys in hand, he headed toward the parking area.

Suddenly exhausted, Louise plopped down on the bleacher beside her aunt to wait.

"You're mad at me, aren't you?" Ethel asked.

Louise turned to look at her. "It's been a long week," she said.

"Clara and I didn't intend that the animals get out of hand," Ethel said. "I didn't mean to leave the names back at my home." Her eyes misted. "I'm sorry if I've been a bother."

Anger drained from Louise, replaced by regret at her

own stubborn pride. She had been so willing to indict Ethel for her mistakes that she neglected to notice her own: She had deliberately withheld forgiveness from a beloved family member.

Her eyes teared, and she took Ethel's hands. "I know, Auntie, and I am sorry if I've been cross, and even more sorry that I've not been willing to think the best of you."

"Sometimes I am so jealous of you, Louise," Ethel said. "We're both widows with our children grown and gone, but somehow you always manage to keep busy and smiling. I suppose your music and students give you purpose, and sometimes I . . . well, frankly, sometimes I feel like I'm just in the way of you and your sisters."

"Oh, Aunt Ethel," Louise said, impulsively hugging her aunt. "I do not want you to ever think that. We are so fond of you, and you, why, you are the youngest-thinking person that I know. What would we do without you?" She raised her eyebrows. "What would Lloyd do without you?"

Ethel blushed, then giggled. "Oh, that man! We do have a good time together. I miss Bob, just as I'm sure you miss Eliot, but it is nice to have a companion. Lloyd *does* encourage me to have fun and stay active. So do you girls."

Louise smiled. Out of the corner of her eye, she noticed Rev. Thompson and Hank wandering around the field. "They're probably wondering why no one has brought them the bowl of names to draw from," she said. "The rest of the crowd too. I'll tell them about the holdup. I'm sure Lloyd will be back soon."

She rose to leave, and Ethel patted her hand, drawing her back. "Thank you, Louise."

"For what?"

"For covering for me when I act less dignified than my age calls for. I can always count on you to keep me in line."

Louise patted her aunt's hand in return, then picked her way down the bleachers to where Hank and Rev. Thompson waited.

Chapter Seventeen

*L*loyd arrived at the field with the fish bowl, which was stuffed to the brim with carefully folded tickets bearing donors' names. Addressing the crowd by means of a wireless microphone, he first announced the total amount of contributions received. The crowd applauded enthusiastically.

"We'll have more than enough for new uniforms and equipment," Rev. Thompson said, leaning in toward the mic so that he could be heard.

Lloyd held the mic in one hand and the fishbowl in the other. "And now, the moment we've all been waiting for. Rev. Thompson, or should I say Coach Thompson, will draw one ticket, on which is the name of the person who will christen our fabulous Little League team. How about a round of applause for the boys? Didn't they play well today?"

Everyone applauded, leaning forward on the bleachers in anticipation.

Lloyd held out the fishbowl, and Rev. Thompson reached into it. He made a great show of rustling the papers around, finally drawing one up from the depths. He unfolded the ticket, and Lloyd held the mic close so that everyone could hear the name.

Rev. Thompson smiled. "The winner is ... Caitlin Cross."

Everyone smiled as the redheaded preschooler made her way to the field, accompanied by her mother, Maura.

"Congratulations, Caitlin," Rev. Thompson said, holding the microphone to the little girl's level.

"Fanks," she said.

"Did you watch the boys play today?"

Caitlin nodded. Evidently the size of the crowd had unnerved her.

"I'm sure you'll want to think about what you want to name the team," he said. "Maybe your mom will want to help you think of some good ones. You can let us know in a day or—"

"I already know the name," she said, smiling as she seemed to remember.

She looked up at her mother, who winced. "I tried to tell her it wasn't a good choice," she whispered, her voice coming across faintly through the microphone.

"I'm sure it's fine," Rev. Thompson said. "Caitlin, what name have you chosen?"

He handed her the microphone, which she proudly lifted so close to her mouth that her words came out loud and clear. "The Acorn Hill Squirrels."

"The Squirrels?" Rev. Thompson looked as though he wasn't certain he had heard correctly.

Caitlin nodded. "Uh-huh. That's what I want to name them."

Jane glanced at the boys now, apparently, known as the Squirrels. Their expressions ranged from disbelief to dismay. And who could blame a fifth-grade boy for being disappointed that his team's new name was not only that of a mean bushy-tailed rodent, but was also a slang word for a goofy person?

The crowd exchanged glances, as stunned as the boys. They applauded halfheartedly. Maura Cross looked mortified.

Rev. Thompson obviously realized the awkwardness of the situation and elected to get the little girl and her mother out of the spotlight. He gestured for Hank to lead them away. "Thank you, Caitlin," he said. "And thank you all for contributing so generously. Our team is grateful to know that we have the town's support. Give yourselves a round of applause."

Everyone clapped a little more enthusiastically this time, then broke ranks to head home. Jane watched as Rev. Thompson joined the players but was instantly pulled aside by some of the parents. Jane sprinted from her seat to join them and was just in time to hear the tail end of their comments.

". . . kind of name is that?"

". . . really kind of embarrassing . . ."

Rev. Thompson held up his hands for silence. "Everyone, please be quiet now. I want you to take a look around you. Do you notice anything?"

The parents looked around curiously, then shook their heads.

"Though I know they're probably not pleased with the name, your sons are not complaining."

Some of the people looked sheepish, but one still looked defiant. "That's because they're too young to understand how silly a name that is," he claimed.

Rev. Thompson held up his hands again before the conversation could begin anew. "They're not too young. And yes, we all know that it's probably not a name any of us would have chosen. But let me tell you all what Caitlin Cross told me before she left. She said she liked the name Squirrels because it reminds her of all the ones she sees at the park. The town's name is Acorn Hill, and acorns remind her of squirrels. She also said that she thought about it a long time, and that she thought squirrels were the smartest animals she knew. They're fast, they're always alert, and they think ahead for the cold winter by storing food during the summer."

A crowd had formed and now listened with rapt attention, and Rev. Thompson smiled. "Caitlin Cross doesn't know much about the game, but she's picked three outstanding qualities for a baseball team: speed, alertness and thinking ahead. Is it really so bad to be named after an animal with those traits?"

The boys perked up, wearing hopeful expressions. Sam Cuttor, a quiet boy, stepped forward. "I have an idea for a logo."

"Let's hear it," Hank said.

"Well, it's a squirrel wearing a ball cap and holding a bat, like he's about to swing at a pitch, but his arms are really big below his sleeves—"

"To show his power," Jane said, caught up in the idea.

Sam nodded. "Right. And he's got a determined look on his face, sort of like a crazy person."

"That would certainly put the fear into opposing teams," Jane said.

Some of the parents were nodding, but others persisted in scowling.

"Oh, come on," Jane said. "It's *fun*. That's what baseball is all about. Fun! Can we please not lose track of that before the season even begins?"

She caught sight of Rev. Thompson and Hank. "I'm sorry," she said. "I didn't mean to speak out of turn. I'm just here to help Pastor Ken and Hank, not run the show."

"Jane's right," Hank said. "Both teams played so much

better after they loosened up and just had a good time. Some of you dads need to lay off the yelling and just let the kids play."

"*Hmmph*," one said. "I'll coach my kid if I want to, and if you don't like it, he doesn't have to play!"

"But I want to, Dad," his son protested. "Honestly, I *do* have more fun when you just let me play and don't try to make me be as good as the players in the major leagues."

The father looked around. He saw that other dads were either nodding in agreement or looking down at their shoes.

"It's human nature for us to want to win," Rev. Thompson said, "but it's just not possible every time. I think we all learn just as much in losing as in winning. Besides, I like seeing the boys try new positions and stances and batting methods. That's what keeps it fun and exciting, in my opinion—not the constant winning."

The father opened his mouth, then closed it again. "Maybe you're right," he finally mumbled. "I don't want the boy to stop playing, after all."

Jane stepped forward. "I had one more idea that I wanted to talk over with Pastor Ken and Hank, but maybe I'd better see if anyone is even interested. I thought it might be fun to attend a professional baseball game together as a team and see what the big leaguers do. Not so that we will expect to hit home runs or throw fast balls like they do, but so that we can see their sportsmanship. And . . ." She glanced at Rev. Thompson and Hank as if asking for permission. When they nodded their approval, she continued. "Frankly, some of you parents need to work on sportsmanship too. I know you're concerned about your boys and want them to play well, but maybe if we can redirect some of that passion toward a professional team, we'll all be in better shape."

Jane took a breath to calm herself. "Well, I've said enough. I'll look into the professional game . . . in case anyone's interested."

Hank stepped forward. "I'm interested. Anybody else?"

All the boys raised their hands. And most of the parents did too.

Jane smiled. "Great. I'll look into getting tickets and I'll give you more details. There's a minor-league team near Philadelphia. Meanwhile, are we still on for building a boat next weekend for the cardboard-boat regatta?"

"That's another excellent way to build teamwork," Rev. Thompson said. "It's the last Saturday we have open before our season begins. We could use the day practicing, but I think it would be a good idea to participate in this boatbuilding project. I hear it's quite challenging to build one on site."

"I also hear that the ANGELs are building a boat on site too," Jane said. "So start thinking about what kind of design you'd like to make."

"Oh, they're just girls," one boy said. "Even if they build a boat, we can paddle faster."

"I don't know," Jane said, crossing her arms. "Girls today are pretty tough. Like I said, you'd better come up with a pretty good design."

"We will," one boy said. "And we'll put our logo on it. Come on, let's go work on it!"

The team, the parents and the coaches headed for Dairyland to celebrate the game. Everyone seemed happier. Rev. Thompson and Hank thanked Jane privately and agreed that attending a minor-league game would be fun and provide a new channel for some of the parents to redirect their energies.

Jane was exhausted and begged off going to Dairyland. As she walked back to Grace Chapel Inn, she passed several people on the street who commented on the game. Vera Humbert, of course, was inordinately proud of her fifth-grade boys. Fred thought that the pitchers of both teams showed great promise. Craig Tracy, though not normally a baseball fan, enjoyed the game immensely. He was sorry that he had to leave early to deliver some flowers for a wedding in Potterston, but he promised to attend future games.

Several people commented on the team's new name, but

not in a derogatory fashion. Jane surmised that they all understood the feelings of a little girl were at stake, and anyway, they had no desire to make fun of the name *or* the Little League team.

She was across the street from the Coffee Shop when she saw Sylvia, Bella and Annie Stoltzfus outside the cafe. They spied her, waved and motioned for her to join them.

Jane crossed the street. "Hi, ladies. What's up?"

"We're going to get something to drink. Would you like to join us?" Sylvia asked.

"Well, thanks, but—"

"It'd be nice if you could, Ms. Howard," Annie said. "I'd like your opinion along with Ms. Songer's and Mrs. Paoli's."

Jane realized she had walked into a serious conversation and didn't think it polite to leave. "I'd be glad to. I could use a large glass of something cold."

Bella led the way inside and waved at Hope Collins before taking a booth. Sylvia sat beside her, and Annie slid into the other red vinyl bench, followed by Jane.

"Hi, ladies. How was the game?" Hope asked.

"Very good," Bella said. "Both teams played well."

"I'm sorry I couldn't make it," Hope said. "I had to work. Though we hardly had any business to speak of. I think the entire town was at the game." She laughed. "That's what I like about Acorn Hill. People here always work together for each other. Even in play. Hey! Maybe I'll suggest that to June as the town motto. 'Working together for each other.' You're still taking suggestions for that Web site, aren't you, Bella?"

She nodded. "We are. We hope to vote on a motto soon, and we're getting some good suggestions in. So you'd better hurry."

"Will do. Meanwhile, what can I get you ladies?"

Jane ordered the largest lemonade available. Sylvia and Bella also had lemonade, and Annie selected a cola. Hope scribbled their orders and promised to return shortly. Before she left, Bella called her back. "Can you add a slice of chocolate pie to my order? My stomach is rumbling for something sweet."

"Sure thing," Hope said, heading toward the kitchen.

"So what's up?" Jane asked.

Sylvia and Bella looked at Annie.

"Ah. This is about you," Jane said teasingly, trying to lighten the moment. "Are you in trouble with these two?"

Annie squirmed, her eyes looking sad behind her extra application of black mascara. "Not exactly. I got a letter from my mother today."

"Not bad news, I hope."

Annie shook her head. "Good news, actually. Remember that boy from my community, Henry Byler?"

Jane nodded. "Your boyfriend, right?"

"Yes."

"Your mother didn't approve of him though."

Annie nodded. "Nobody did. He was causing some trouble, going on his *rumspringa*, you might say, even though he stayed in the community. Some kids do that. In fact, very few kids actually do as I did and leave the community." She looked thoughtful. "Of course, some do and never come back."

"That's what we've been discussing," Sylvia said.

Jane held up her hand. "Maybe you'd better tell me about Henry Byler first, Annie. What's the good news?"

She took a deep breath. "My mother sent me word that he's decided to be baptized. That means he wants to be Amish. For life. I know Henry, and he doesn't do anything without believing in it. If he was testing his freedom before and he's decided now to settle into the faith, then I know it's real."

"That seems like a good quality in a man," Jane said. "I admire that about the Amish community. Their letting young people decide for themselves, I mean."

Hope reappeared, setting down their beverages and Bella's pie. "Anything else, ladies? Anybody else want a snack of any kind?"

Everyone shook her head. "No thanks," Jane said. "But you can keep the lemonade coming. It was just warm enough outside today to make me really thirsty. I feel like I ran a mile, though I was just standing in the sun."

"It's been an interesting spring all right," Hope said, refilling Jane's glass. "Well, you ladies let me know if you need anything else. Otherwise, I'll tend to my other customers."

Sylvia leaned forward, clearly wanting to get the conversation back on track. "So you can see Annie's dilemma. She's liked this young man for a long time. They've talked about marriage, so she assumes he feels the same way about her, right, Annie?"

The girl nodded. "At least he *did*. That was when I lived with the Amish. If I decide to stay in the outside world, that won't be possible. Once he gets baptized, he can't marry anyone who isn't Amish. And I'm certain he'll start looking seriously for a wife because he's the right age. He'll want to start settling down."

"It's a difficult decision," Sylvia said. "Can you give him up, Annie? Not to mention your mother and the rest of your family. I'm not trying to influence you, but you need to look at all sides of this."

Annie twisted a paper napkin between her hands. "I know it's a lot. I would be giving up everyone I've known and loved my entire life."

"Just tossing this out," Jane said, "but some would say you'd be losing your freedom and the chance to control your own life if you went back. Do you agree with that?"

She leaned forward. "I've learned in school that with freedom comes responsibility, and that it's about individual expression, like what color eye makeup I choose every morning. But I don't know that I agree. Mam always said that freedom came in the *Ordnung*, the rules that we people live by. The Bible does say that we are to be a peculiar people," Annie said. "The Amish take that literally and have no problem with the rest of the world thinking about them that way."

She put her hand over her heart. "I know all this here, but I'm really confused right now. I don't know what to think, but I know I have to make up my mind soon."

"Bella, what do you think?" Sylvia asked. "You've been silent about the whole issue."

Bella looked up from her pie. She put down her fork, glanced at Jane, then turned her attention to Annie. "I don't know if anyone's told you, dear, but I was raised Amish."

Annie's eyes widened. "You were?"

Bella nodded. "I left the community a long, long time ago. My family is still in Ohio."

Annie propped her elbows on the table like any interested teenager. "What happened?"

Bella smiled. "My young man was not Amish. He was English."

"*Oooh*, that's so romantic," Annie said, rolling her eyes. "You gave up family for the love of your life."

"In a way," Bella said slowly. "I used to help my mother bake goods to sell, much as you help your mother with her quilts. One day I met a woman and her daughter who ran the

English bakery nearby where my mother sold her food. I got to know them well, and when I was an older teen, I met the woman's son, who would become my husband. We were never alone together, but he and his sister—and sometimes his mother—would talk to me about the Bible. I went home and started reading for myself, and some of the verses seemed counter to what I had always been taught."

She smiled, remembering. "I had been baptized, but I had not married, though I had been asked. Then Carmine told me that he and his family were moving, and that he didn't want to leave without me. He knew it was asking a lot, but he wanted me to marry him and move with him and his family and start a new bakery business."

She drew a deep breath. "I went home that night and prayed. I knew it would mean giving up my family, for they would have to shun me if I left the faith. I was in love with Carmine, but enough to leave my community? After a night of prayer, I realized the answer was yes. In the morning, I told my parents and brothers and sisters of my decision and I joined the Paolis. Carmine and I married." Tears filled her eyes. "And I never looked back."

"But how could you do that?" Annie whispered, stunned by the story. "How could you leave everyone who you loved?"

"Because not only did I love Carmine, I realized after reading the Bible for myself that I did not agree with all of the Amish teachings. All these years, I have relied not only on Carmine's love but on that knowledge. I even changed my first name to reflect my new life."

"What was your given name?" Sylvia asked.

"Katie." She ate a bite of her pie. "I changed my name to Bella not only because it fit well with my new Italian surname but because it means *beautiful*. And that is how God sees me."

No one said anything for a long time. Annie stared at the tabletop. Jane was touched by Bella's story. Imagine leaving a family forever. Jane had left her family, too, but with the opportunity to return at any time. Daniel Howard would have welcomed her home no matter what she had done, just as Ethel or her sisters would have. Bella had left her family, but also the only faith tradition she had ever known.

Jane wiped away a tear that had formed in her eye. Bella laughed softly and handed her a napkin from the chrome dispenser. "Come on, everybody. I didn't mean to make you feel so maudlin. Annie, it is your decision. I won't lie. It may be the most important decision you make in your life. I have told you my story, but I won't influence you further. I suggest that you pray. The Lord is always the best guide and advisor."

Annie nodded. "I will," she whispered.

"Would you like for us to pray for you now?" Jane asked.

Annie smiled. "That would be good."

Jane held out her hands. Annie accepted one; Sylvia took the other and reached for one of Bella's hands. Bella completed the circle by taking Annie's free hand. Jane smiled at their little group, then she lowered her head. The background noise of the Coffee Shop faded as Jane began.

"Dear Lord, Annie has a decision to make that will affect the rest of her life. No one can help her except You, and we ask that You give her wisdom. Let her hear Your voice clearly, so that she will know the right path to take. Thank You for loving all of us and watching over us each and every day. Help us to trust You in every aspect of our lives and to be Your light in whatever worlds we live, whether Amish or English. Amen."

"Amen," the women echoed softly.

Jane lightly squeezed Annie's hand before releasing it. When they raised their heads, Jane saw tears in Annie's eyes.

Chapter Eighteen

*T*he rest of the weekend passed uneventfully, and soon it was Wednesday. The Campanellas continued to work on their boat and take occasional tours around the area. Lauren had talked her family into driving to Philadelphia that day to check out the conservatory where Louise had studied and her husband had once taught.

Louise was eager to hear their impressions, and she found an excuse to wait on the front porch for their return. She had volunteered to do some knitting for a women's auxiliary fundraiser at Potterston Hospital, so she passed the time working on a pale-pink baby blanket.

While she knitted, she reflected that it had been a long time since she had used baby blankets. Her only daughter, Cynthia, was over thirty years old now and living in Boston, where she was a children's-book editor. Thinking of the Campanellas at the conservatory reminded her of when she and Eliot had lived in Philadelphia with a young Cynthia, the three of them snug and happy in the Greek Revival home they had restored.

Time went by so fast. It did not seem so long ago when she had knit a similar blanket for Cynthia. Being a mother was the greatest joy in Louise's life, even if Cynthia no longer needed her in the same ways that she had growing up.

God was so good to have brought her full circle to her home, to her sisters and to Grace Chapel Inn. The inn was not just a source of income but a joy and a blessing as well. Helping their guests by providing a comfortable and friendly place for them to stay had become a vocation for her and her sisters. It was an even greater joy and blessing to have renewed her relationship with Jane and Alice in ways that they had never experienced growing up.

Precious, too, was the renewed relationship with Ethel. Louise said a silent prayer thanking God for revealing her impatience with the older woman. She could easily see herself in Ethel's place in a decade or so, needing someone else's patience with her frailties and confusions.

"Hi, Mrs. Smith," Lauren said, bounding up the steps of the front porch, the rest of the family close behind.

Louise started. She had been so deep in her thoughts that she hadn't noticed the car drive up. "Hello. How was your trip?"

"Fantastic. I'm so glad you told us about the conservatory."

"We were most impressed," Allison said.

"And Philadelphia was way cool," Sidney said. "I wouldn't mind visiting Lauren there at all."

"It's definitely one of the top schools on my list," Lauren said.

"Be sure to let me know when you reach a final decision," Louise said.

"I will," Lauren promised. "I'd better go work on my costume for the regatta on Saturday. See you later, Mrs. Smith."

"We'd better do the same," Allison said. She smiled at Louise, then followed her oldest daughter into the house. The rest left as well, and Louise was alone once more.

She started knitting again, smiling. Seeing another young person involved in music gave her deep pleasure, even if it was not one of her own students.

⌒

That night, the sisters gathered in the living room after Alice's meeting with her ANGELs. Louise brought her knitting, Jane practiced calligraphy at a portable lap desk, and Alice read aloud from one of a series of books that the sisters enjoyed.

When Alice's voice grew weary, she set the book aside for a while. "Any news about Annie Stoltzfus?" she asked.

Jane shook her head, setting her calligraphy work aside as well. She rubbed her eyes. "I talked to Sylvia today, and she told me that Annie hasn't made a decision yet."

"That's a difficult choice for anyone to make," Alice said. "Whatever she chooses will affect the rest of her life."

Louise nodded. "I would hate to sway her, but I simply can't imagine a life with no formal education, no musical instruments and so little personal freedom."

"But I can't help thinking that family is the most important thing in the world," Alice said softly. "What would she do without hers?" She sighed. "What do you think, Jane?"

"I don't know. I once thought like Louise, but now I'm not so certain. It's not a decision I'd want to make."

"Nor I," Louise said. "Fortunately, my biggest decisions now involve the town Web site, and even then, Hank and Bella do the choosing. I'm available for second opinions only."

"When will the Web site be up and running?" Alice asked.

"Hank has a basic site up now that can be accessed, he says. But it's nothing to look at. 'Bare bones,' I believe was the way he phrased it."

"What about the town motto?" Jane asked.

"I think Hank and Bella have collected all the submissions they're going to receive. They'll be posting them at Town Hall—and on the Web site for those who are electronically inclined—within the next few days."

"Have you see any of them?" Alice asked.

Louise shook her head. "I'm going to the mayor's office tomorrow after I stop by the library. Nia will be back in town on Friday, so it will be my last day to make sure everything is in order."

"I hope things are going better," Jane said.

"They are," Louise said. "Malinda has finished up the paperwork and is making sure the library is in tip-top shape for Nia's return."

"Ethel and Clara have been behaving themselves?" Jane asked.

Louise nodded. "They have been restricted to book checkout only. There is much less chance of their causing trouble that way. They've also been keeping busy working on their boat for the regatta on Saturday."

"Really? What's it like?" Alice asked.

"They won't say. They claim they want it to be a surprise," Louise said. "I don't know what it is about this weather, but this spring has certainly brought out the sports enthusiasts in our town."

"I got tickets for the Squirrels to attend the minor-league game tomorrow night," Jane told them. "You both are invited if you'd like to attend."

Louise shuddered. "I can only take baseball in small doses."

"And I have to work late tomorrow," Alice said. "I do

look forward to seeing the Squirrels play soon, though. It's nice to see young people enjoying sports."

"I'm not sure that a cardboard-boat regatta could rightfully be called a sport, but it's definitely something else the Squirrels are interested in. How about your ANGELs, Alice? Are they ready for the big race on Saturday?"

"Some of them are. The others are getting cold feet, I'm afraid. We spent most of the evening working on our boat design, and only half the girls were enthusiastic. We drew straws to select the five girls who would actually ride in the boat."

"Boat design?" Louise asked. "Didn't you tell me they planned to build a boat on site rather than in advance?"

Alice nodded. "Vaughn Campanella told me that it would save a lot of time during the competition if the girls would figure out in advance what design they wanted to follow. I've tried to help as best I can, but I'm afraid I don't know much about boat dynamics. How about the Squirrels, Jane? Have they worked on their design?"

"Somewhat," she said. "They're all interested in the competition, but they're so confident they're going to win that I'm afraid they've lost interest in thinking about the kind of boat they want to build. If you ask me, they have a little too much faith that they're going to slap something together and automatically win due to brute strength."

"And my girls are just the opposite," Alice mused.

"They're giving a lot of thought to the project. They want to be sure they build something that will float and that they can paddle to victory."

Thursday morning Louise headed to the library. She had popped in only once since the animal incident and had relied, as she'd reported to her sisters, on good words from Malinda Mitschke. Indeed, things did seem to be running smoothly. Patrons milled about in the hushed library atmosphere. The air—finally—smelled only of books and nothing untoward, and every book and magazine seemed to be in place.

Ethel manned the checkout desk. When she saw Louise, she smiled. "Hello," she said in a hushed tone. "May I help you with anything?"

"I just stopped by for a moment," Louise said.

"Checking up on me?" Ethel winked.

"Not really, Aunt Ethel. You seem to be doing fine. Are you still enjoying your library work?"

Ethel thought for a moment. "Sometimes. Although it's occasionally slow and a little on the boring side. There are other people who want to volunteer, too, new people, so I may see if I'm needed somewhere else in town. Like at Vera Humbert's school. Maybe I could help some of the teachers there."

Louise smiled. "I'm just glad to see you back to your old self."

"You mean that useless feeling I had?" Ethel waved her hand. "That disappeared. It always does."

"You mean you've felt that way before?"

"Lots of times. It happens at my age. You'll find out as you get older, Louise. Sometimes you just need to shake things up a little, then you feel like your old self again."

Louise winked. "The next time you feel that way, Aunt Ethel, let's just take a trip together, all right?"

"Sure thing. I'd better get back to work. Good to see you, dear."

"You too."

Louise walked toward the administrative offices but met Malinda in the reference section. "I wasn't expecting to find you here. I thought you'd be in your office."

Malinda smiled broadly. "Not today. I'm spending my time where I'm happiest. Out here in the stacks with the books and the patrons."

"The paperwork is done?"

Malinda nodded. "Thank goodness. And just in time. Nia will return tomorrow, and I couldn't be happier about that."

"It was a huge responsibility for you while she was gone," Louise said.

"I wish I had done better, but the silver lining is that the library is spotless. Thanks to you and Alice."

"We weren't the only ones who helped." Louise glanced

at the carpets. They did look exceptionally clean. The book-shelves, too, were free of dust and fairly sparkled, thanks to Ethel and Clara's ill-conceived reshelving project.

"I want to thank you for all your help," Malinda said. "Not only cleaning up after the, er, messes, but for your encouragement. A lot of people would have said that I was doing a fine job, that accidents happen, but you were willing to be a true friend and suggest that I take a leadership class. I'm going to look into that when Nia returns."

"You *did* do a fine job under the circumstances," Louise said. "You believed that Clara and Ethel would do a good job, and they let you down. The good thing about mistakes is that if you can learn from them, they'll be worthwhile."

Malinda nodded. "I've certainly learned my lesson. I've learned that people often do need more supervision than you might expect . . . *and* that you should never allow animals into a library—even if it rains."

"Indeed," Louise said with a chuckle.

After she left the library, Louise headed toward Mayor Tynan's office. Hank and Bella were huddled in front of Bella's computer, just as she had hoped.

They smiled when they saw Louise enter. "Wait till you see what Hank's done," Bella said. "The Web site is going to be wonderful."

"It's just a beginning," Hank said, ducking his head modestly. "Take a look at it, Louise. We need another opinion."

At the top of the page was a photo of City Hall and a short paragraph about Acorn Hill. "We'll probably change that once we've selected the town motto," Hank said. "Right now it's just filler."

Below the photo was a map showing the location of Acorn Hill, and below that were clearly delineated sections: Information, News, Quality of Life and Upcoming Events. The Information section had links to a phone directory and the latest town-council agenda. The News section featured construction reports, and the Quality of Life section was linked to information regarding health care, housing, library, recreation, Realtors, religious groups and other interests. Upcoming Events listed important activities soon to take place. The Squirrels' first game, scheduled for the following week, was listed at the top.

"That might seem a little self-serving, since I'm one of the coaches," Hank said.

"It's the next big event in this town. I think it is quite appropriate," Louise said.

At the bottom of the page was a row of small photos, each one of an area business. Louise saw the *Acorn Nutshell*, the Coffee Shop, the Good Apple Bakery, Zachary's, Sylvia's Buttons and others.

"I'm not sure about that part," Hank said. "We've

already received a lot of response from interested businesses, and I'm afraid we won't be able to cram them all on the bottom of the page. I think we'll probably pick one representative photo to link viewers to another page listing all the businesses."

"That sounds like a wonderful idea, and I am certain you know best about these things," Louise said.

"Overall, though, as someone who's admittedly not a professional critic of Web pages, how do you like it?" Bella asked.

Louise smiled. "I think it looks splendid. But what about the town motto? Have you received a lot of suggestions?"

Bella drew a shoebox from under her desk. The container was half-full of paper slips. "Hank and I have gone through these over and over, and we're not certain that there's anything that really grabs us."

"Nothing that really captures what Acorn Hill means to its citizens," Hank added.

"At one time you mentioned asking Lloyd about an original town phrase we could use," Louise said. "Did anything come from that?"

Hank and Bella shook their heads. "We even combed some of the oldest historical records and nothing turned up that would be useful for today. The town *does* have a wonderful old history," Bella said. "It would be a shame not to honor that in some way."

"We'll post what we have this afternoon and vote on Saturday. Lloyd wants us to move on this thing . . . the motto and the Web site," Hank said. "Carlene listed the contributions we already had in yesterday's *Nutshell*, so most people have seen them."

"Oh yes, I remember," Louise said, "and you are right. Nothing stood out or grabbed me. There was nothing that symbolized the town as most of us feel about it."

"Here's the list we've accumulated so far," Bella said. She handed over a piece of paper on which she'd typed all the suggestions, which included a few that had not made yesterday's newspaper. Louise scanned the list, frowning. Most of them were vaguely worded or clichéd, like "Acorn Hill—A Good Place to Visit, a Great Place to Live."

"I can't imagine that we really want to focus on the tourist aspect of Acorn Hill," Louise said. "We're more of a way station between larger towns."

"Yes, and even if it's edited to read 'A Great Place to Live,' well, it just sounds a little . . . flat," Hank said. He sighed. "I'll go ahead and post these on the Web site for now, though. Meanwhile, if you have any suggestions, let us know."

"I don't know that I can contribute anything, but I'll certainly give it some thought," Louise promised.

Soon after her stop at Town Hall, Louise headed home. As she was walking up the path to Grace Chapel Inn, she heard unusual sounds coming from the carriage house. Louise could not see anything, so she headed over there to find out what was going on.

Ethel had lived in the carriage house for the last ten years, and it was as trim and tidy as the day she'd moved in. Louise walked around back and found Lloyd Tynan and Clara Horn laughing as they worked on their cardboard-boat for the regatta.

Lloyd glanced up, saw Louise and boomed, "Don't come one step closer, young lady! No spying on our boat!" He moved in front of their work to block her view.

Louise automatically backed up. "I was not spying, Lloyd. I just heard noises and wanted to check on them."

"He knows you're not a spy, dear," Clara said, moving in front of the boat beside Lloyd. "But we want this to be a complete surprise for everyone on Saturday."

Louise heard a squeal and realized that Clara had Daisy in her baby carriage behind the boat. "Is she all right?"

"She's fine," Clara said, rushing to the carriage nonetheless. "She's just excited about the work we're doing."

Lloyd relaxed. "We're expecting your aunt to return at any moment so that we can put the finishing touches on our project."

"I saw her at the library," Louise said. "I'm sure she'll be along soon. And I promise I didn't see enough to have a clue about your surprise."

Lloyd squinted good-naturedly. "You're sure?"

Louise nodded.

"Well then, I guess we can let you go," he said.

"Thanks," Louise said, shaking her head in amusement. Saturday and this boat regatta could not come soon enough.

Louise half expected to find the Campanellas working on their boat, but there was no sign of the family, only a piece of paper taped to the back porch that said Keep Out. "They must be finished," she murmured. "Ah me, more secrets to keep."

Jane and Alice were not at home. She drifted to her father's study and sat down in the leather chair behind the desk. Glancing around at the many books on the mahogany shelves, she spied one that caught her attention.

It was a book of Latin quotations. She rose to remove it from the shelf, then sat back down in the chair. The feel of the book in her hands and the smell of must tickling her nose reminded her of times long ago. She had been inexplicably drawn to this book when she was a child and would curl up in one of the library's chairs to study it while her father worked on his weekly sermon. The unfamiliar words had seemed wise and almost magical in their obscurity.

She opened the book and flipped through the pages. She spoke aloud some of the Latin phrases, remembering how awkward they had sounded on her tongue when she was a child. They sounded much less mysterious to her now, after having studied Latin in school.

"*Ipsa scientia potestas est.* Knowledge itself is power." Louise sighed. "I'd like to tell that one to Annie Stoltzfus. *Ora et labora.* Pray and labor. That could be the motto of the Amish indeed."

She scanned the page, reading a few more aloud. Then she read a phrase that made her heart quicken. It was lovely. It described Acorn Hill so well that it could, indeed, make a fitting motto.

Clutching the book, she headed for the phone in the reception area and dialed Bella's extension at Lloyd Tynan's office. "Bella?" Louise said without preamble. "I think I have one more suggestion for the town motto. It's Latin, but everybody knows *quidquid latine dictum sit, altum viditur.*" She laughed, then when she heard silence said, "That means, 'Whatever is said in Latin sounds profound.' But in this case, I think it's true. The phrase fits Acorn Hill to a T. Just listen."

Chapter Nineteen

*B*ella thought the phrase was wonderful, as did Hank when she repeated it to him. They told Louise they would add it to the list, and that they considered it a top contender.

Hank took the phone from Bella's hand so that he could talk to Louise himself. "So much better than 'A Great Place to Live,'" he said.

When Louise hung up the phone, she was feeling pleased.

Jane had arrived and walked into the reception area from the kitchen. Seeing Louise's smile, she asked, "Who was that?"

"Bella and Hank. I called them about the town motto."

"I hope Hank doesn't get too involved with that right now. He should be getting ready to go to the game."

"Game?"

"The Squirrels are going with their parents to the minor-league game, remember? We're leaving soon after the kids get out of school."

"Oh! Yes. How could I have forgotten?"

"Sure you don't want to go?" Jane winked.

"No. Thank you." She glanced at her watch. "Actually, it's time for me to prepare for a piano lesson."

"Well, I've got a date to hear an organ play 'Take Me Out to the Ball Game.' As far as other music goes, we might also have a little sweet chin music."

Louise blinked. "You mean a violin?"

Jane laughed. "No, Louie. You see, when a pitcher throws a ball high and inside to brush back a batter, it's called chin music. Get it?"

"I'm afraid I don't. However, chin music or not, I hope you all have a wonderful time at the game."

"Thanks. And now, I'd better hurry up and change. I need to wear something more comfortable for watching baseball on a warm afternoon."

Alice came home from work late in the afternoon. She entered through the back door and noticed that Jane had left a note on the table.

> Gone to ball game. Louise and Alice—there's a plate
> of cold cuts and cheese in the refrigerator and bread
> and crackers on the counter for your dinners.
>
> Love, Jane

"Thank you, Jane, for being so thoughtful," she whispered. "I'm too exhausted to fix anything."

She did, however, put the teakettle on the stove. A warm cup of herbal tea was what she needed right now; that and to put up her feet. It had been a busy day at work, without a moment's rest.

When the water had boiled and chamomile tea steeped in the teapot, she contemplated taking a cup into the living room, where it was more comfortable. At the moment, however, she was too tired to move, so she sat down on a kitchen chair and propped up her feet on another. No doubt Jane would scold her for putting her feet on the kitchen furniture, but what her younger sister didn't know wouldn't hurt her. Just this once.

The tea was steaming in the cup, and Alice had barely taken an exploratory sip before a quiet knock sounded at the back door. "Come in," she called.

Annie Stoltzfus entered, followed by Sylvia. The teen's eyes were scrubbed clean of makeup, as was the rest of her face. She wore a simple knee-length denim skirt and a white cotton blouse. "Is Jane here?" Annie asked.

"No, sorry, I'm the only one here. Jane went to the game with the baseball team, and I believe Louise is having coffee with a friend. Would you two like to sit down? I have a pot of hot tea ready to share."

Sylvia glanced at Annie, who nodded. "That would be lovely," Sylvia said.

Alice got two more cups and saucers from the cabinet, set them on the table and poured the tea. She sat back down, resting her feet on the floor this time. "May I ask what brings you here looking for Jane?"

"It's not a secret," Sylvia said. "Annie just wanted to talk to Jane because she had a good conversation with her, Bella and me at the Coffee Shop the other day."

"I heard about that," Alice said. "Jane filled us in on your dilemma." She paused. "I hope you don't mind that she did. She knows that we all are concerned about you."

"It's all right," Annie said. "I know you sisters are close and share just about everything. That's the way I am with my family."

"You must miss them a great deal," Alice said gently.

Annie nodded. She twisted her hands in her lap. "It's an awful decision to make. Sometimes I wish I hadn't come here at all. Maybe it would have been better not to have seen what the English world was really like."

"Why?"

"Then I wouldn't know what I've been missing. Of course, there are some things I wouldn't mind missing." Her eyes twinkled. "Some of the kids my age here in Acorn Hill have so many . . . things. And yet they lack so much." She shook her head. "I'm probably speaking out of turn."

"That's all right, Annie," Alice said. "What things do you think English teenagers lack?"

She sighed. "Family, for one. If their parents aren't divorced, everyone in the family is going in five different directions at once. We do that sometimes too, at home, but it's always with the same purpose—for the family. Here, kids . . . well, they're going to soccer practice and their mams are working. They hardly ever sit down together for dinner, and if they do, it's usually from a fast-food restaurant."

"You're right about that," Alice said. "The English world must seem to you to move at rapid speed."

Annie nodded. "Computers, cell phones, television, all these gadgets—how does anybody have any time to think?"

Alice smiled and shrugged her shoulders. This was a question she frequently asked herself.

"And the way kids treat other kids," Annie said, obviously wound up on the subject of the English world. "Boys and girls together with no thought of marriage. We encourage that, too, but it's more courting than just having a good time. Henry and I wouldn't have spent much time together unless we thought we might be serious about each other."

She clamped her mouth shut as though she had said too much. She looked down at her hands in her lap.

Sylvia smiled at the girl fondly. Then she turned to Alice.

"You're familiar with the news Annie got about the boy she was hoping to marry?"

Alice nodded. "He's decided to be baptized. Is that right, Annie?"

"Yes. And so I've been praying for the past week about what I should do. Do I let him go, let all of my family go, to live in the English world, or do I return and become a permanent part of the Amish faith?" She looked directly at Alice and smiled. "But I've made up my mind."

Annie's eyes sparkled, and Alice knew there would be no turning back for Annie Stoltzfus, whatever her choice.

Sylvia clasped her hand. "I know it was a tough decision," she said, her eyes wet with tears.

Annie nodded. "I came here to tell Ms. Howard, to tell all of you, what I decided." She drew a deep breath. "I'm choosing to return. I want to be baptized."

Alice smiled. "I can see by the look of peace on your face that it was the right decision."

"It wasn't an *easy* decision," Annie said, "but yes, I believe it is the right one."

"You had so many options to consider. Was there one thing that helped you more than anything?"

Annie smiled. "My family. They mean the world to me. They *are* my world. Televisions or cars or phones will never be more important than the people I love most."

"And Henry Byler?" Sylvia asked.

"I realized that I can't turn my back on him either. I liked hanging out with the Franklin High kids, and most of them are very nice. But I know now that I'm just not interested in the latest CD or movie or shopping at the mall. I know I would always miss the little things—my mother's kitchen, harvest time, the smell of the soil in the spring and knowing that you rely on its eventual bounty, my brothers and sisters…" Her eyes welled with tears. "I can't imagine life without them…or Henry."

Sylvia put her arm around Annie, and Alice reached over and touched the girl's hand.

Annie sniffled. "I will miss you all and hope that you'll come to visit Mam and me. And Henry, once we're married," she said shyly.

"Of course we will," Sylvia said. "I hope you'll continue to help your mother with the quilts, but if not, I'll make a point to see you when I'm in Lancaster."

"Will you and your sisters do the same, Alice?"

She nodded. "We don't get to Lancaster often, but we will try to see you whenever we do." She refilled their cups of tea. "Will you come back later when Jane's home from the baseball game?"

Annie shook her head. "I've asked Sylvia to take me home today. I can't wait to get back."

"Then you have definitely made the right decision,"

Alice said, smiling. "When you know where your heart is, there is your home."

On impulse, Annie leaned over and hugged Alice. "Thank you so much."

Alice returned the embrace, wrapping her arms securely around the young woman. "Why, whatever for?"

Annie pulled back, smiling. "You let me talk. You encouraged me to say what I thought. That's why you remind me so much of my grandmother. She did that too."

Alice smiled and patted the girl's hand.

"Will you tell Jane that I did get to see *The Lord of the Rings* with Sylvia?" Annie asked. "All three movies. It took forever, but it was worth it. If I wanted to watch movies on a regular basis, I would want ones like that." She paused. "I felt all week as though I've had a burden that no one else could carry. I identify with poor Frodo."

Annie brightened. "Please tell the Campanellas that I'm sorry I'll miss the regatta, but I'm sure that they and their boat will look wonderful."

Sylvia rose. "We'd better go, Annie. I'm sure your mother will be glad to have you back at the supper table tonight."

Annie rose as well. "Good-bye, Miss Howard. I enjoyed meeting you and your sisters. Please thank them for me for putting up with my foolishness." She smiled. "I was so glad to throw away that eye makeup. It took too long to put on every morning, and it really wasn't that good looking. I hope other girls my age will realize that soon enough."

"I'm sure they will," Alice said. She drew Annie into another hug. "May the Lord bless and keep you."

"May He bless you as well," Annie said, hugging her back warmly.

"May He bless us all," Sylvia finished, joining them in the hug.

The Squirrels caravanned to the game. Rev. Thompson drove a couple of boys and their fathers, and Jane rode with Hank. Between them on the seat was his player's glove, and she glanced at it questioningly.

"You never know when you might catch a ball," he said, shrugging.

When they arrived, Jane was enchanted by the small, somewhat crumbling old minor-league stadium. She knew it didn't have nearly the splendor of Citizens Bank Park, where the Philadelphia Phillies played, but it obviously represented a lot of memories and baseball lore. She could also tell by the boys' awed expressions that it looked like a palace to them. Many of them had never been to a professional baseball game.

They were not so awed, however, that they turned down the parents' offers of cotton candy, peanuts and popcorn. By the time everyone had rendezvoused and reached their seats out in left field, the boys, parents and coaches were loaded down with treats and souvenirs.

One sheepish father even sported a home-team pennant. "It reminds me of being a kid," he said. "My dad always bought me one."

Hank clutched a bag of roasted peanuts. "How about you, Jane?" he asked. "Are you going to buy a pennant? Maybe a bobble-head doll?"

"Good heavens, no," Jane said, laughing, "though I must confess to a need for something spicy. Nachos with plenty of jalapeno peppers for me, even if the cheese is, *ugh*, processed."

Smiling, Hank cracked a shell and popped the peanuts into his mouth.

A local country-western star belted out "The Star-Spangled Banner."

"Play ball!" Hank yelled immediately afterward, and everyone else took up the cry.

The organist played a lively introduction, and the home team took the field one player at a time. The crowd roared as each position was announced. When the third-baseman's name was called, the crowd cheered and rose to its feet.

Jane stood beside Hank and yelled over the applause, "What's so special about Jackson Street?"

"He holds several major-league batting records, including home runs, but he's here on assignment. He had an injury in spring training, and he's rehabbing here. It's an honor to see him play in person. I'm sure he'll enter the National Baseball Hall of Fame one day."

The boys quickly got into the spirit of the game, as did their parents. Jane was delighted to see the overbearing dads yelling at someone else for a change. They also took an occasional opportunity to point out a stellar play or something that would help their sons improve their game. With the pressure on the professionals instead of the boys, however, Jane knew it was advice well given.

Except for when he was shelling and eating peanuts, Hank kept his glove on during the game. Jackson Street came to bat, and Hank pounded his right fist into his glove. "Come on, Street! Let's see that sweet stroke. Put that tater up in the bleachers!"

Amused at the banter, Jane felt herself caught up in the excitement. She cupped her hands around her mouth and yelled, "Come on, Jackson, we want some action. Hit a homer!"

Street swung at the ball and missed. The crowd groaned. "Ouch," Hank said.

The pitcher looked at the catcher, nodded his approval at the called pitch, then threw the ball with all his might. Street stepped forward on his leading left foot, then swung in a beautiful arc.

Crack! The ball sailed toward the left-field bleachers where the Squirrels sat. Jane watched as Hank, as if in slow motion, rose from his seat and held his gloved hand high in the air. When he lowered the glove, the crowd was cheering wildly. Jackson Street had hit a home run, and Hank Young, coach of the Acorn Hill Squirrels, had caught the ball.

The Squirrels jumped up and down, torn between watching Street round the bases and staring at the ball in Hank's glove. Hank held up the ball in triumph so that the crowd could see.

"You caught it!" Jane yelled. "You caught it!"

"Yeah," Hank said, breathless. "I wonder if I can get it signed."

An elderly uniformed usher appeared at the end of the row. "Nice catch."

"Yeah," Hank said, all smiles. "Say, do you think I could get it signed by Mr. Street? I'm the coach of this Little League team here, and it would mean a lot to all of us."

"I'll see," the usher said. "Why don't you give me the ball and I'll take it down to the dugout?"

Hank held it away suspiciously. "Are you sure you'll come back with it?"

The usher laughed. "I promise I will."

Hank reluctantly turned over the ball to him and watched nervously as he headed for the dugout.

"He'll bring it back, Hank," Jane said. "Don't worry."

Hank couldn't take his eyes off the usher, who handed the ball to a trainer in the dugout. "*Uh oh*, I was afraid of that.

It'll probably get lost with the other baseballs in there." He slumped, dejected. "Oh well, at least I know I caught it."

He and Jane went back to watching the game. Street appeared at bat again an inning later, but struck out. The home team, however, was winning.

The usher reappeared, his hands empty, but he was smiling. "Mr. Street said that if you can wait after the game, he'd like to see you and your entire team in the dugout. He's a former Little Leaguer himself, and he'd like to meet some of the kids today."

The Squirrels went wild. Hank grinned. "Tell Mr. Street that we'll be there."

The game couldn't end fast enough. At last the visiting team made the last out.

Hank reminded everyone to help gather up the remnants from the game—pennants, programs and leftover popcorn. Hank led the way down the bleachers toward the team dugout. When they reached a security guard at the field, he introduced himself and explained the situation.

"Sorry." The man shook his head. "I can't let you into the dugout. Anybody can say that."

"But I caught the home-run ball," Hank said.

Jane could feel his disappointment and that of the boys and parents.

The man shook his head again. "I'm sorry, but that doesn't mean Mr. Street agreed to meet with you."

"But—"

At that moment, the usher appeared. "It's okay, Carl. Mr. Street is expecting these people."

"That's all the approval I need," the security guard said. "Right this way."

He led them down into the dugout where the players' bench was located. Empty sports drink cups littered the floor, along with streams of water. "I hope that's not spit," Jane whispered to Hank.

Except for a bat boy who was gathering up equipment, the dugout was empty. Suddenly, from out of the tunnel under the stadium, the great Jackson Street appeared. "Hi, everybody. Sorry to keep you waiting. Who caught the home-run ball I hit?"

Everyone was in shock, from the kids on up to Hank, who stood openmouthed.

Rev. Thompson nudged him, smiling. "This young man did."

"Here's the ball back," Jackson said, holding it out for Hank. "I've already signed it."

"Th-thank you," Hank whispered, scarcely looking at the ball as he accepted it. He cleared his throat. "That was quite a hit. Your shoulder must be feeling better."

"It feels great. So did the home run." He glanced around at the boys. "So who are all these fine fellows? I understand you're a Little League team, right?"

One boy stepped forward. "We're the Squirrels, sir, and it's a pleasure to meet you."

"Squirrels, huh?" Jackson asked. "How'd you come up with a name like that?"

When no one else spoke up, Jane quickly explained. "So to a preschool girl, Acorn Hill and Squirrels just seemed to go together."

Jackson rubbed his chin. "Makes sense to me. You boys should be proud of your name, then. Sounds like you have the whole town behind you. It's important to play together well, whether you win or lose. Always be a good sport."

The boys nodded, speechless.

"And you dads." Jackson turned to them. "Support your sons, but give them room to make mistakes. Play catch with them during the week, but once the game starts, let them do their thing. And no yelling afterwards, okay?"

The fathers nodded, speechless as well.

Jackson smiled, bringing his hands together. "Now. Who'd like an autograph or to pose for a picture?"

The boys came to life, swarming the famous player. The parents who had brought cameras readied them and promised to share photos with those who had not. Jane even got her photo taken with the player, and he kissed her on the cheek for the shot.

After they finished and said good-bye to the ball player,

the Squirrels left the dugout, fairly walking on air. They were the last ones to leave the stadium and would have stood around talking if the security guard had not encouraged them to move toward the parking lot. On the walk back to the car, Jane studied the photo of herself with Jackson Street on the digital camera's screen. "This is so cool. Wait till Alice and Louise get a load of this."

"I got a photo too," Hank said, then held up the autographed baseball. "Not to mention this."

"What are you going to do with it, Hank?" Rev. Thompson asked.

Hank paused thoughtfully. "I'm going to put it in a protective case. I don't want anything to mar Jackson Street's signature."

⌒

The next morning, while she was eating breakfast, Louise got a phone call from Malinda Mitschke. "Nia will be in this morning around ten o'clock," she said. "Could you possibly be here then too? I'd like a little backup, so to speak, to explain what happened."

"I can be there," Louise said. "Don't worry, Malinda. It'll be fine."

"What was the phone call about?" Jane asked.

When Louise explained, Jane said, "Oh, good. I want to come too. I want to talk to Nia."

"About anything special?" Alice asked.

Jane glanced at them both, and Alice smiled. "Ah, the secret you're supposed to keep. The one that has something to do with why Nia stayed extra days in Pittsburgh?"

Jane nodded. "Yes, and I've a feeling it may not be a secret much longer, and I'd like to be there to find out for certain."

"Alice, would you like to come too?" Louise asked. "It seems a shame for you to miss out on the fun."

"Why not?" she asked, grinning over her cup of tea.

The sisters bid good-bye to the Campanellas, who were holed up on the back porch with last-minute preparations for the boat. The regatta was the next day.

Louise wondered if Lloyd, Clara and Ethel had their boat ready too.

At the library, they found Nia standing at the checkout desk with a clearly nervous Malinda.

"The reports look wonderful," Nia was saying. "You really knocked yourself out on these." She glanced up. "Jane! Louise! Alice! How lovely to see you all. It feels like I've been gone forever."

Jane gave her a hug. "Any news for us?" she said, smiling.

Nia smiled back, noting the bewildered looks on the others' faces. "What Jane is referring to is my boyfriend. I thought he might pop the question this past week, and yes, he did."

Jane squealed with delight, but before she could say anything, Nia held up her hand. "Marriage would have meant that I'd have to leave Acorn Hill, though, and I'm not ready to do that. I told him I'd rather continue our commuting relationship for now. He said if this town meant that much to me that he'd try to find a job in the area. It won't be easy, but we'll continue to see each other when we can until he can find something around here. We decided not even to consider ourselves officially engaged just yet."

"That's still wonderful," Jane said. "And secretly, of course, I was hoping you'd stay."

"I have to say, though, that I'm starting to wonder if I'm needed here after all." She smiled at Malinda. "Everything's in such good shape, with all the reports finished. All the books are in order and the computer up to date."

She glanced around the library. "And the carpet's cleaned and all the shelves dusted." She clucked her tongue, turning to the sisters. "Malinda told me it was all due to Ethel and Clara, and all I can say is that it was very thoughtful of them to take care of those things in my absence. They are truly wonderful ladies. It's a shame more libraries don't take advantage of their seniors' help." She put her hands on her hips in pretend petulance. "I have a feeling I wasn't missed around here at all."

"Oh, you were missed, Nia," Louise assured the librarian. "Believe me, you were."

"What do you mean?" Nia glanced at the women who were sharing knowing smiles.

Malinda hesitated a moment, then, after Louise gave her an encouraging nod, gave Nia a weak smile. "Maybe you'd better sit down."

Chapter Twenty

$\mathcal{S}$aturday morning, everyone at Grace Chapel Inn was awake early, ready to head out for the regatta. The Campanellas barely touched the breakfast Jane made for them. They were eager to ready their boat for the trip to Riverton.

"How on earth are you going to get it there?" Jane asked.

Vaughn smiled. "We rented a pickup yesterday and built a scaffold. We'll tie the boat down to that, and with some careful driving, we'll make it."

"I'm glad the ANGELs are building their boat on site," Alice confided to Louise and Jane after they'd watched the Campanellas leave.

"I must admit that my curiosity has gotten the better of me," Louise said. "I can hardly wait to see all the boats."

"We caught glimpses of the Campanellas' boat while they were working on it," Alice said, "but it will still be interesting to see it in the water."

"I wish Annie could have been here for the regatta," Jane said, a tinge of sadness in her voice. "I know that she did what she thought was best and what God was calling her to do, but I can't help but think that she'll miss so much."

"I try to focus on everything she will gain," Alice said. "She will always have her family."

"And apparently a husband," Louise said. "We should be happy for her."

Jane brightened. "Yes, you're right. Meanwhile, let's get this party started and head for Riverton and those cardboard boats."

Alice's ANGELs, as well as the Squirrels, drove separately to Riverton. The regatta would be held at an Olympic-size pool, with racers required to start at one end and make a complete lap around the perimeter to the finish line. Those who built their boats on site would be given the necessary materials and a special area to create their vessels.

The town pool, opened early for the event, teemed with regatta participants and onlookers. Women at long tables by the entrance gate allowed the participants to enter for free, since they had already paid a registration fee. Spectators paid a small amount, which, like the other fees and profits, would go toward the local nature center. A local rock radio station, which promised to promote the event throughout the day, blared overhead.

A concession stand sold cold drinks and snacks. Cardboard boats were lined up at angles around the sides of the pool, with some participants in costumes, and some—

perhaps prophetically—dressed in swimwear. Whether spectators or participants, people laughed and joked, gearing up for a fun day in the sun.

After they paid the entrance fee, the sisters said goodbye to one another and went their separate ways. Jane headed out in search of the Squirrels, while Alice looked for the ANGELs. It turned out that they were in the same area, because both groups were building boats on site. The Squirrels laughed and joked among themselves while the ANGELs huddled together, going over last-minute plans.

Alice was pleasantly surprised to see that the girls seemed to have a working blueprint and were already discussing how they would decorate the finished project.

"Let's make a halo," said one.

"No, wings," said another.

Ashley Moore, who seemed to be in charge, said, "Let's just see what we have left over. We only get cardboard, duct tape and plastic."

The first events were for those who had already built their boats. The girls headed toward the sides of the pool to watch the early races. The first ones were for five-man teams. Every participant had to wear a life jacket, and each used an oar to paddle.

The girls were delighted by the creativity of the participants. Some of the boats were painted in dramatic colors. One was painted like a patchwork quilt, another in shiny silver with sharp black trim, and still another was painted yellow and shaped like a banana, down to the Chiquita label on its side. Both male and female crew members had dressed like Carmen Miranda, complete with headdresses of plastic fruit, bright tropical sarongs and sandals.

Other boats were more fancifully designed. One resembled a pirate ship with a crew that looked like they'd stepped straight out of the movie *Pirates of the Caribbean*. They wore colorful jackets, knee-length pants and scarves around their heads. One man even had a fake parrot attached to his shoulder.

"Oh, look, there are our guests," Alice said, pointing out the Campanellas to the girls.

The Campanellas' boat looked wonderful, shaped like a boat from ancient lore. It bore the name *Grey Ship* on its side, which, Alice reminded the girls, was the name of the ships in *The Lord of the Rings*.

The family had dressed up as major characters from the novel and movie—Vaughn as Gandalf wore a long white beard and white wizard's robe, and Allison as Frodo was in short brown pants, vest and white blouse. She wore a large gold ring on a chain around her neck.

The girls dressed in long flowing dresses. Lauren and Sidney wore pointed elfish ears to identify them as Galadriel and Arwen. Marsha was dressed as the maiden warrior Éowyn, an aluminum-foil sword at her side.

As they stepped next to their boat, the audience cheered. The Campanellas waved regally, playing their roles magnificently. When the starter's pistol went off, all the contestants in that race jumped into their boats and paddled toward the finish.

"Go, *Grey Ship!*" Alice and the ANGELs yelled.

The Campanellas battled a sleek speedy-looking boat for the lead. They rowed with all their might, pulling hard for the finish line. Those on the side of the pool screamed for their favorites.

Ten yards from the finish line, *Grey Ship* surged ahead. "The winners!" the announcer cried over the intercom, and everyone cheered and applauded.

Alice let out a sigh of relief. "Oh, thank goodness." She put her hand over her heart. "I'm breathless."

"They won!" the ANGELs danced, as though it were a personal triumph.

"Wait, listen," Alice said, putting her fingers to her lips. "They're saying something over the loudspeaker."

"Now it's time for our on-site builders to begin," a man's voice boomed. "Would all the participants please report to the building area?"

The girls rushed back to the area they'd staked out, just in time to be handed their allotted cardboard, box cutter, pencil, duct tape and plastic. "What's the plastic for?" Ashley asked the official.

"You can put it on the inside or outside," he said. "It's for making the boat a bit more waterproof."

The girls consulted their design to make sure the plastic would not interfere.

Alice noticed that the Squirrels were holding up their cardboard in a playful manner, laughing and roughhousing.

"Do you think we can beat them?" Ashley asked her.

"Of course you can," Alice said. "Remember what you said at the meeting? Just have faith."

"Builders, get ready!" the official announced. "You'll have two hours to make your boat, then we'll race them to determine the winner. Ready, set, GO!"

The girls scrambled to mark the cardboard with their design. Alice watched them mark, cut, fit together and finally line their boat with plastic and tape. She was amazed that a seaworthy vessel actually seemed to take shape under the girls' hands. But would it float?

While the participants worked on their boats, the officials announced other races. More five-man teams competed against each other, though Alice scarcely noticed, so intent was she on observing the ANGELs. She managed to catch the last of one race, where the pirate ship barely edged past the banana boat at the finish line. The crowd roared with laughter when one pirate pretended to feed his fake parrot plastic fruit from the headdress of one of the Carmen Mirandas.

At least ten other teams worked furiously to build their

boats by the two-hour deadline. Most of them appeared to be children's teams, but here and there a few adults worked together.

Alice glanced over at the Squirrels. They seemed to be squabbling over their design, but one look from Rev. Thompson and they stopped arguing and went back to work. Alice heard and caught occasional glimpses of other races under way, but she concentrated on what the girls were doing, and the two hours went by swiftly.

The official blew a whistle. "Time's up!" he said to the boatbuilders.

"We made it," Ashley said as she and the other girls collapsed dramatically in heaps on the ground. They had not only finished their design, they had indeed managed to add a pair of duct-taped angel wings to the side of the boat.

"Take your vessels to the starting line," the official said. "It's time to race!"

The five girls who were going to race strapped on the required life jackets and carried their boat upside down over their heads, paddles in hand, their energy renewed. Alice followed behind them, her heart racing with excitement for the team.

They put their boat into the water alongside the other three competing boats, including the Squirrels'. The boys' boat had gaps barely covered by the plastic. Alice was not certain that it would float, much less race.

"Everybody ready?" the official called.

"Ready!" the teams shouted back.

"Faith, girls, faith," Alice said.

"On your mark, get set, GO!"

The four teams shoved off, leaping into their boats and beginning their furious paddling for the finish line. The crowd went wild, cheering their encouragement.

The Squirrels jumped out to an early lead, primarily a result of their furious paddling. The ANGELs held a respectable second, paddling as hard as they could. "You can do it!" Alice whispered, her words lost in the screams of the onlookers.

Suddenly, halfway through the race, the Squirrels' boat began to break apart. Though the boys paddled as though their lives depended on it, the ANGELs began to overtake them. The boys watched in desperation as the girls passed them.

Ashley Moore, in the stern, looked back. Alice saw an expression cross the girl's face that could only be described as determination. She stopped paddling. Instead, she reached her oar out behind her for the boy in the bow of the Squirrels' boat to hold on to. He accepted it, and his crew continued to row what was left of their rapidly deteriorating ship.

Rowing with all their strength, the ANGELs not only crossed the finish line first, but pulled the Squirrels along as well. The crowd cheered loudly.

Alice raced to the finish line to congratulate the girls. An official was there to welcome them as well. "That was some fancy paddling," he said, his voice booming over the wireless microphone he held. "Are these boys your friends?"

Ashley nodded, and he held the microphone out to her, evidently figuring her for the spokesperson of the group. "They're our town's Little League team, and we're proud of them," she said.

The official cornered one of the Squirrels. "Looks like you had a little trouble with your boat, son."

"We sure did. It was nice of the ANGELs to help us," he said, smiling his appreciation in their direction.

"Angels? Oh, *that* explains the wings on your boat," the official said. "Why are you called the Angels?"

"We're a service group from Grace Chapel in Acorn Hill," Ashley said. "Our leader is Miss Howard here, and she encouraged us to participate in this event. We didn't think we could do it."

"Well, you certainly did do it," the official said. "And here's your trophy to prove it."

A young woman brought out a gold-colored trophy and handed it to Ashley, who passed it around to the other girls. They each held it for a moment, then passed it back to Ashley, who lifted it up high. They motioned for Alice to join them, then they mobbed her in a group hug. Louise and Jane joined them as well.

The announcer was already calling the next race, one for three-man teams. Alice checked the starting line. A local celebrity newscast team stood beside a sleek black racing boat. Another crew consisted of three men all dressed like Napoleon. Another group stood alongside a boat constructed to look like a piano lying on its back.

"I bet Lauren loves that," Louise murmured.

"Look!" Jane said, almost yelling to be heard over the crowd's shouting for the race to begin. At the far end of the pool, by a cardboard-boat painted to look like a house of red bricks, were Ethel, Clara, Lloyd…and Daisy the pig. Ethel and Clara were dressed up as pigs, complete with rubber snouts and pointed pink ears. Lloyd was dressed as the Big Bad Wolf.

Alice laughed and, catching Jane's eye, saw that she was laughing too. The boat looked wonderful. Who would ever have guessed that those three could pull off such a clever idea?

"Ready? Set?" The starter put the whistle between his lips and blew.

The crowd cheered, but at the sound of the whistle, Daisy squealed in fear. Ethel, Lloyd and Clara managed to hop into the boat and picked up their paddles, prepared to race to the finish line. But Daisy, porcine legs straight out, lunged over the edge of the boat and landed with a splash.

"Daisy!" Clara threw down her paddle, and grabbed for the pig. Her motion tipped the boat precariously.

"Careful!" Ethel yelled over the din of the crowd. She dropped her own paddle and tried to steady the boat, but it gave a mighty wobble, then tipped the three unceremoniously into the shallow water of the starting line. They came up spluttering but unharmed. The other contestants paddled farther and farther away, nearly half-finished with the race.

The three looked at each other, their costumes dripping, the boat tipped over and soaked. Lloyd was the first to smile. Then he laughed, his black rubber nose and gray wolf ears twitching even as they slid from his head. Their own rubber noses askew, Ethel and Clara looked at each and burst into laughter as well.

Daisy paddled happily over to Clara, and the crowd applauded. The pet nuzzled her owner as if to express her regret.

"Daisy," Clara said, scooping her up to hold her close. "I'm so glad you're all right."

"Thank goodness Daisy is okay," Alice murmured to Jane. "It's almost as if she jumped in on purpose."

"I think you're right," Jane said. "Look, that pig is smiling!"

When the regatta was over and everyone split up to go home, the sisters, exhausted, piled into Louise's Cadillac. "That was much more fun than I imagined it would be," Louise said. "I was quite happy not to participate, but to simply watch all the wonderful entries."

"Who knew that Ethel and Clara and Lloyd could be so creative?" Jane asked. "They looked like they were having the time of their lives. Even Daisy seemed to have fun. She certainly enjoyed all the attention she got after the boat sank."

"It is a wonder, though, that Clara did not get a life jacket for it in the first place," Louise said. "She does baby that animal to no end."

"All's well that ends well," Jane said. "At least they got the *Titanic* award for the best sink. And your ANGELs really came through, too, Alice."

She nodded. "They certainly did. We all had our doubts about the competition, and I'm proud of them just for entering."

Louise glanced at her watch. "We have just enough time to get home and change. Hank, Bella and Lloyd are going to announce the winner of the town motto competition at Town Hall at five o'clock."

When they reached the inn, the sisters saw the Campanellas getting out of their rented pickup. They had changed from their costumes back into regular clothes, and the boat was nowhere to be seen.

"Congratulations on the win," Jane said. "You guys looked great! But...what happened to the boat?"

Vaughn smiled. "Cardboard only holds up so long in water. We had to throw it in the Dumpster they provided in Riverton."

"All your hard work," Alice said. "What a shame."

Allison shrugged. "There's always another project and another adventure awaiting us. Meanwhile, we had a lot of fun, and we got a lot of digital photos to remember it by."

"Why don't you join us later tonight for dessert and coffee? We'd love to see some of those photos," Jane said. "Meanwhile, we've got to go to a town meeting. Make yourselves at home."

"Don't mind if we do," Vaughn said. "We're exhausted from the work. For once, we're going to take it easy."

The sisters freshened up and headed for Town Hall. Quite a few other citizens had gathered there. Lloyd talked about all the hard work that had gone into the Web site, singling out Hank, Bella and Louise for creating it from scratch.

Hank handed Lloyd a piece of paper, and Lloyd smiled. "And now comes the moment for which we've all been waiting. The new town motto. I have it on good authority that this was the last submission, but it was the overwhelming favorite among the voters." Staring at the paper, he cleared his throat. "*Ahem.* This will take a little practice, since it's in Latin. But the winning phrase is '*Respice, adspice, prospice,*' which means, 'Look to the past, the present, the future.' Louise Howard Smith was the contributor of this motto. Louise, please join me."

Everyone applauded as Louise stood next to Lloyd. "Tell us why you chose this," he said.

Louise looked out at the people of her beloved town and smiled. "I chose the motto because it truly seemed to fit our town. We in Acorn Hill have a strong historical past, we enjoy our lives together now, and I have no doubt that we'll continue to do so in the future. Tying the past, present and future together in our motto seemed appropriate."

She paused and smiled out at the audience. "In addition, though the town might prefer the translated version for the Web site, we all know," she paused for effect, "anything said in Latin sounds dignified."

The music of hearty laughter punctuated the end of her explanation.

About the Author

The late Jane Orcutt is the best-selling author of thirteen novels, including *All the Tea in China*. She has been nominated for the RITA award twice. A proud wife and mother of two sons, she lived in Fort Worth, Texas.

Tales from Grace Chapel Inn

Back Home Again
by Melody Carlson

Recipes & Wooden Spoons
by Judy Baer

Hidden History
by Melody Carlson

Ready to Wed
by Melody Carlson

The Price of Fame
by Carolyne Aarsen

We Have This Moment
by Diann Hunt

The Way We Were
by Judy Baer

The Spirit of the Season
by Dana Corbit

The Start of Something Big
by Sunni Jeffers

Once you visit the charming village of Acorn Hill, you'll never want to leave. Here, the three Howard sisters reunite after their father's death and turn the family home into a bed-and-breakfast. They rekindle old memories, rediscover the bonds of sisterhood, revel in the blessings of friendship and meet many fascinating guests along the way.